ALL IN GOOD TIME

LEGACY SERIES
BOOK 6

PAULA KAY

DEDICATION

To Dawn.
Thank you for your friendship, love and support.

CONTENTS

ONE

Isabella Dawson wiped the vomit from her chin as she sat back against the bathtub. God, why did she have to get so worked up about everything? She was well prepared with her speech. Her parents had made sure that she'd had plenty of practice, listening to her recite the words that she'd be saying in front of the entire school in just two short hours.

She looked toward the knock at the door and smoothed her long dark hair back as she stood up to brush her teeth.

"Izzy?"

She rolled her eyes at the nickname. "Yeah, Mom."

"Iz, are you okay in there? Do you want to come out and do the speech for Dad and me one more time?"

"I don't think so."

No, I think I got it. Please leave me alone. And please stop calling me Izzy.

She hated the nickname that she'd grown up with, and for the past few months she'd been really trying to get her parents to stop calling her Izzy—she wanted to be taken seriously at Harvard and she didn't think Izzy was going to cut it for a future lawyer.

Leo, the owner of the Italian restaurant that they loved to go to, always called her Bella whenever he saw her. It made her smile —she liked it better than Izzy—but she wasn't sure that she was a Bella either.

She was a serious young woman—that's the way her teachers described her anyway—Isabella Dawson—high school valedictorian and future Harvard law student.

No, she was way too serious to be a Bella.

She peered into the bathroom mirror wondering if she had some make-up that could cover the darkness under her eyes. She hadn't actually worn make-up since she'd first tried it two years ago. She'd begged her parents to let her wear it and they'd finally allowed her to once she'd turned sixteen. But then she always felt that they disapproved so she'd quit wearing it after only one week —besides, it always ended up running down her face during track practice anyway, so it was really more of a bother than anything.

Her mother told her that she didn't need make-up—that Isabella was a natural beauty—but Isabella always noticed a certain look on her mother's face when she talked about her beauty. She'd always told Isabella that there were more important things than good looks—and they'd certainly raised her to think much more of her intellect and natural talents than anything else.

She splashed some cold water on her face and stared into the dark brown eyes of her reflection looking back at her.

You got this, Isabella. It's no big deal. Just do it like you've practiced a hundred times.

And even though she was feeling anxious, she knew that she'd pull it off. That her parents would be out in the seats watching her, their smiles wide with pride at the perfect speech that their daughter had delivered. They'd hug and kiss and then her father would take them out for an expensive dinner that was the very rare occasion within the Dawson household.

She sighed as she dried her face off and prepared to walk out of the bathroom. She desperately wished that she had time for a quick run, but she knew that she didn't. If she could make it past her parents—who she knew were waiting to accost her with all of their positive words—to her bedroom, she'd take a few minutes to do one of her journal exercises. That seemed to help lately.

She hadn't shared with her parents that she'd been meeting regularly with Ms. Carlson, the high school guidance counselor, for the entire last semester of her senior year. One day Ms. Carlson had come into the bathroom while Isabella had been throwing up. It was during finals and her nerves had been nearly shot from the anxiety of all the tests—the tests that she'd aced, of course, but her preparedness didn't seem to help when it came to her need to do well. After a lengthy discussion back in the counselor's office, Isabella had finally convinced her that she didn't have an eating disorder, but Ms. Carlson had been firm about Isabella setting up a next meeting with her. And that was how their regular Wednesday meetings came to be.

Isabella fell a twinge of sadness now as she thought about the final meeting that she'd have with the woman who had become quite an important part of her life over the past months. Even though graduation was today and school was officially over, they had one more meeting scheduled for next week.

Relieved that her parents had been in the other room when she'd come out of the bathroom, Isabella made it to her bedroom, where she pulled her journal out of her bedside table. She'd been keeping a journal for as long as she could remember—she'd been writing for as long as she could remember too. She'd gone from scribbling beginnings of stories on paper, to writing a full-size novel on the new lightweight laptop that her parents had given her for Christmas the past year. But almost no one knew about her intense love for writing. She had the feeling that the knowledge of it would somehow worry her parents—that somehow it would become a bigger thing than what it was. And she wasn't kidding herself about a career as a writer. That was just a fun idea. Her goal throughout high school had been that she would become a successful lawyer one day, and everything that she'd worked so hard for had landed her a spot in one of the best schools in the country.

Her journal had become more of a therapy tool for her lately. Ms. Carlson had helped her to realize that this intense amount of pressure she'd been heaping on herself was more than not just healthy—that it was really affecting her quality of life—a big life that she had in front of her—the big life that everyone wanted for her. She tried not to think about her parents as she turned to the task at hand.

At the top of the page she wrote the big scary thing—the task that was making her feel anxious—*valedictorian speech at graduation*. Worst-case scenario—she'd completely space out on the whole speech, everyone would laugh at her and her parents would be incredibly embarrassed.

Next question—how likely was this and could she die as a result? She smiled as she thought about the question Ms. Carlson had asked her one time when she was feeling particularly nervous about one of her track meets. Running track did have some possible physical outcomes that weren't nice, but she didn't really see death as being one of them—considering that she was a healthy young teenager anyway. So, the likelihood of death resulting from her forgetting her speech was zero, and the probability of her forgetting her speech was very low as well. If Isabella was anything, she was a girl who was prepared.

And what was the best-case scenario regarding the speech she was about to give? That she'd be able to deliver a passionate speech that would move the students, the teachers, and her parents. That somehow the words that that she'd spent hours agonizing over would inspire everyone in the auditorium.

That somehow the words that she spoke would inspire her.

TWO

Isabella looked out at the sea of faces, most of whom she knew, but very few that she'd be able to call friends. She glanced down at her notes as she prepared to wrap up, but more out of habit than anything else. She had every word memorized and she also knew how to deliver a perfect speech. Four years on the debate team had taught her that.

Yet today felt different. She felt like she was listening to someone else speak—that it was someone else's voice that she heard in her ears.

"So as we go forth on to the next phase—this next adventure of our lives—let us do so boldly and with a great passion that can't be held back."

Was Harvard her great passion?

She glanced over at her parents, their smiles wide, each the picture of what a "beaming with pride" parent should look like. For a moment, it was all worth it—the anxiety, the pressure that she'd been heaping on herself to make them proud. But then she had to muster a deep and, most likely, unnoticeable breath to finish her speech with the same bravado.

It wasn't that she wasn't excited about Harvard or didn't think that she'd excel there. She had no real reason to doubt herself, with many years of past successes behind her. But it seemed like something was missing for Isabella. She didn't seem to have the same excitement as most of her classmates when it came to talking about her next step. For her, it was just more of the same, only probably much more intense.

She squared her shoulders and smiled widely at the clapping audience, stepping out from behind the podium to take her seat for the remainder of the ceremony. She glanced over at her best friend, Thomas, who was sitting a few rows back. He gave her a thumbs up and mouthed the words "awesome job." She grinned at him and thought that she might ask her parents if it was okay for Thomas to join them for their celebratory dinner afterward.

She and Thomas had met one another in the fifth grade when they'd been paired together as lab partners in science class, and they'd been best friends ever since. Thomas would be taking a year's deferment from entering NYU in order to travel, something which drove Isabella slightly insane on the one hand and left her a bit awestruck on the other. Isabella couldn't imagine being as close with anyone as she was with Thomas.

Before she knew it, it was time to move the tassel on her cap as the graduating class was officially announced. The entire auditorium erupted into shouts as she tossed her cap high into the air along with her classmates, laughing as Thomas came up behind her to swoop her up in a giant hug.

"We did it, Iz!"

She hugged him around the neck and whispered in his ear as she saw her parents walking toward them.

"Don't let my parents hear you calling me that. I'm trying to get them to stop." She laughed and Thomas winked at her.

"Well, you two, how does it feel to call yourselves graduates?"

"It feels pretty great, Mr. Dawson," Thomas was quick to reply, moving away from Isabella just a bit to give her parents room to get close to her.

Her father leaned over to give her a kiss on the cheek. "Your speech was so good, baby."

"We're so proud of you." Her mother reached over to give her a hug, but not before Isabella saw her wipe the tears away.

"Thanks. It does feel pretty good."

"*And* to be done with that speech, I bet." Thomas gave her a look as if he wasn't sure if he should mention it—she'd been stressing about it for days around him too, so she was pretty sure that *he* was the one who was ready for it to be behind them.

"Yes, you can say that again."

"Now you won't have anything to stress about until—hmm—next week maybe?"

He was joking with her but she saw the disapproval on her mother's face. Her mother didn't like to joke around when it came to the things that Isabella felt anxious about. These were all important things in her parent's eyes, and Isabella had to learn how to cope better with her nerves. Isabella didn't think they really understood at all how she felt about it, but it was never really up for debate—just something that she had to continually work on until the anxiety finally went away.

"Are you ready to go?" her mother asked her.

Thomas and her father were chatting quietly off to the side.

"Mom, would it be okay if Thomas joined us?"

But she could tell by the way her mom's face changed as soon as she'd asked the question that it was a family dinner.

"Oh, I don't know, honey. I think your father wants to celebrate with just us. Thomas's parents probably want to celebrate with him as well, don't you think?"

Isabella nodded, disappointed, but not surprised. Her parents liked Thomas—although they had opinions about his carefree attitude—but they were big on intimate family celebrations. She didn't bother to tell her mother that Thomas's parents had already asked Isabella to join them for a celebration dinner tomorrow night. The two already had plans for lunch the next day also, so they'd do their celebrating together then.

"Thomas, I'll see you tomorrow then? Around one?"

"Sounds good."

Thomas gave her a hug, and Isabella was left standing with her mom squeezing her arm on one side and her father already taking off toward the parking lot.

"Let's go. I'm sure the restaurant is going to be busy. You want Italian, right?"

Isabella nodded her head. Italian food was always her go-to favorite when they went out—it had been ever since she was a kid —ever since she'd found out that she was at least half Italian.

She flashed to a memory of doing a school project on ancestry. It was one of the first times that she'd had a true conversation with her parents about her adoption. She'd always known that she was adopted. They'd made sure that she knew how much they'd wanted her from the moment she was born—that she'd been special, chosen to be their daughter.

Her mother had often commented on Isabella's dark thick hair, unruly as a child and now one of Isabella's favorite physical features—if she'd been forced to name one. So she'd grown up looking nothing like her mother, who was of Irish descent, or her father, who was also fair-skinned with blue eyes.

It had never really bothered Isabella that she was adopted until years later when she'd tried to have another conversation with her mother about it. Isabella had been about thirteen at the time and for some reason, she'd started thinking about her birth mother a lot. She didn't know exactly why, but she felt apprehensive talking to her mother about it—about asking for information. Her mother had made it clear to Isabella that it was a topic that was off limits—not so much by her words as by her strange reaction— she'd been uncomfortable, and Isabella hated seeing her mother like that.

So, she'd put the whole thing out of her mind. She was a

Dawson, daughter of Emily and Richard Dawson and that was the end of it back then.

It was Thomas who'd gotten her thinking about it again only recently, when she'd turned eighteen a few weeks ago. She'd been looking for a good time to have the conversation with her parents, but things had been so busy with the end-of-the-year madness, that she'd not had a chance yet to bring it up—and she was dreading it to a certain extent. Isabella didn't like to rock the boat in her family and she'd done a great job of being an excellent daughter for all of her life.

THREE

Like clockwork, Leo appeared at the door to greet the Dawsons as soon as they arrived at Angelica's. The restaurant was named after Leo's wife, who was also in charge of the kitchen. Isabella loved to watch the couple interact whenever her family dined at the restaurant. Their banter—which sometimes seemed to border on petty arguing—in Italian was mesmerizing to her.

"Bella, congratulations." Leo kissed her on each cheek as Angelica came up beside him to do the same.

"Tonight, dessert is on us."

Isabella laughed and felt her face grow warm at the attention. "Thank you. You're so sweet."

"Come, come. I have a nice table for you over here."

They followed Leo back to a corner of the dining room and settled in.

After they placed their orders, Isabella noticed her parents giving one another a look.

"What?" Isabella grinned at them. "Do you two have something to say?"

"Well, yes, actually. We have a little surprise for you, honey," said her father, motioning to her mother, who was suddenly grinning from ear to ear.

"We'd like to contribute to a car for you. You're going to need one for school in the fall—"

"—so that you can easily come visit us, for one thing," her mother cut him off.

"We probably have close to fifteen thousand saved up," her father finished.

"And we figured, with what you've got saved, that should be enough to cover something new that would be reliable and safe for you to drive," said her mother.

Isabella looked at the two of them grinning at her from across the table. She'd been saving to buy a used car ever since she'd been old enough to work a summer job. She'd never in her wildest dreams thought that her parents would be able to help her buy a car. Her family was far from wealthy. They might be considered middle-class, but barely, she was sure. Her mother was a high school teacher at one of the public schools and her father was a social worker.

"No, you can't do that. What about your trip?"

She knew that her parents had been saving for a trip to Europe for the past few years. Neither of them had been out of the country, and they had it in mind for their twenty-fifth wedding anniversary, which was coming up in the next year. Isabella knew that they'd been able to earmark the money that they had been putting toward her expensive private high school, an expense that they'd insisted was well worth the financial sacrifices that they'd had to make as a family over the years.

Her father glanced at her mother, reaching over to take her hand. "Mother and I've decided that our trip can wait a few years."

Isabella was shaking her head in response to his words. "No—"

"Izzy—Isabella, you've worked so hard and we're so proud of you, honey." Her mother reached across the table for her hand. "We want to do this for you."

Isabella could already feel the guilt eating at her, like something ravaging her stomach. She didn't want them to do this for her. They'd sacrificed so much as it was. For some reason, she could never shake the feeling of being undeserving. It was certainly not anything that her parents had ever put on her. They always wanted her to be happy. She knew this. But they did have expectations for her. Isabella knew that everything they'd put into her education would lead to an ultimate outcome—her success as a lawyer. They'd always wanted the best for her and for her to have much more than their modest upbringing. They'd worked tirelessly for that. And Isabella always felt that she owed them her success.

She tried to focus on her food, but she felt the tears threatening just behind her eyelids. She turned her attention back to her parents. "Well, we'll see. Maybe we can find something used for a good price. I don't have to buy a new car. That way I could get my wheels and you two could still go on your trip."

"Okay, we'll see, honey."

"Let's talk about this summer," her father said. "When does your internship start?"

Isabella had been accepted to a very sought-after internship program by a local law firm. She'd mostly be filing and doing other secretarial-type tasks, but it would look very good on her resume and it was definitely a firm that she'd like to develop a relationship with—and it was a paid internship, which made it a no-brainer for her.

"It starts in just over two weeks." She twisted her pasta around her fork as she thought about the direction she intended the conversation to go. "And my writing class starts next week, but it's in the evenings."

Her parents looked at one another, and she didn't miss the glance. As much as they did support all of her educational endeavors, for some reason, they'd never been able to get behind anything that had to do with her writing. If Isabella had to guess, it was because her mother had majored in English and then ended up becoming a teacher. They wanted more for Isabella than to be a teacher. They didn't have to say it in so many words. It was just a fact that she'd always known.

"What's the class again?" her mother asked.

"It's an advanced creative writing class."

She'd excelled in all of her writing classes at school. Her teachers had seen her talent and one of them had even entered one of her short stories into a national contest just last month. She was still waiting to hear the results, but it was really something that she'd done just for fun.

Writing was her outlet. It was the one way that she could truly express herself, whether through a made-up character or her journal writing. She had to laugh sometimes, because she'd been called a good communicator by so many of her teachers and her debate team coach—it was one reason that she knew she'd be a good lawyer—but when it came to communicating with her parents, she was lousy at it. Mostly she just held everything in, which was probably why she had all of the anxiety issues that she did.

She didn't want to discuss the writing class with her parents right now. The night was supposed to be a celebration, and she didn't want to spend another moment of it feeling like she was going to bust into tears.

"Anyway, I'm sure it will be fine. I can handle the one class and the internship, no problem."

"Well, just be certain that it's not going to interfere, because you really want to think about how the things you're choosing to do will look on your resume one day. Just keep your focus, as you have been doing such a good job of, and there's no doubt in our minds that you're going to be at the top of your class next year as well."

Isabella nodded her head. She'd had this same conversation with her father at least twenty times in the past few months. She knew exactly what she was doing. She had to wonder sometimes if that was what had been causing her so much anxiety.

She couldn't help but smile as she thought about the irony of it all. She'd figure it all out. She always did.

FOUR

Thomas had that look on his face. Isabella enjoyed it when he was in one of his moods, but she also found it hard to understand at times. Thomas didn't have to work at being relaxed. It was just his nature to not be serious.

"Well?"

"Sorry, what?"

Thomas laughed and kicked her lightly under the table. They were sitting in the usual corner booth of the diner where they'd been meeting for years. The restaurant was almost exactly the same distance for each of them—.6 miles—and they'd been coming here together just as soon as they were old enough to make the walk by themselves.

Thomas's parents had allowed him the privilege long before Isabella's parents had made the concession. The one time Isabella had gone against her parent's wishes, to sneak to the diner—at Thomas's prodding—her mother had freaked out, calling the police because she thought someone had snatched up ten-year-old Isabella right out of their house.

"Iz, I was just saying that you really should meet me."

"What are you talking about?"

"I'm talking about you meeting me somewhere in Europe at the end of the summer—before you start school. Ya know, it's called summer vacation for a reason." He laughed.

Thomas was leaving to start his travels in the middle of August, and Isabella felt sick when she thought about saying goodbye to him.

"You know I'm going to be very busy this summer—with the internship and everything."

"And?"

"And what? That's the truth."

"But you have a few weeks before school starts. Iz, you already told me that."

She nodded.

"So just admit that its not the real reason you won't meet me."

"Okay, so what? I can't help it if the idea of flying petrifies me." She returned a light kick under the table. "Do you want me to die from a heart attack on my way to see you?"

"Come on. You, more than anyone I know, probably can quote exactly what the statistics are, Isabella. You'll be fine. Besides, don't forget that I know the truth." He reached over to grab her hand across the table, causing her to flinch at his unexpected touch.

Thomas was the only one who really knew about her dreams —the only one who knew that she had a stack of books in her closet that covered country after country that she longed to experience one day.

She nodded and squeezed his hand. "I know. You're right. You are. Let me think about it, okay?"

Seemingly satisfied with her response, Thomas let go of her hand to gesture to the table across the room. "By the way, I think you have an admirer."

"What?"

She looked in the direction that Thomas had pointed and just as quickly looked back at him, feeling her face grow warm. Isabella wasn't used to male attention, even though Thomas was forever pointing out the guys that he said thought she was gorgeous. He said that was one of the qualities that he loved most about her. That even though Isabella was by far the prettiest girl in their class —his words, not hers—she was the most unassuming girl that he knew. He said the other guys liked that about her as well.

Isabella didn't know about all that. What she did know was that she did not have time for a serious relationship, so she was never really that interested in talking to new guys. Besides, she had Thomas to hang out with, and she wouldn't trade the time they spent together for anything or anyone.

"Oh, stop. No one's looking at me."

"Sure, whatever you say, Ms. Ice Queen." He winked at her and she bristled just a tad.

"Stop. I'm not. Do you really think I have time for guys right now?" Thomas was looking at her with that funny expression again—the one that made her uneasy because she knew he was about to say something serious to her.

"Isabella, you really need to loosen up, ya know. No one our age should be so serious all the time."

"I'm not serious *all* the time."

"Most of the time you are."

"But not always with you. Come on, Thomas, you know that."

"I do. I do know that. I'm not trying to give you a hard time, honest. I just care about you. I want you to be happy, home fry." He laughed.

"Speaking of fries..."

"Double with extra chili and cheese?"

She nodded. Now that track was over, she hadn't been so strict with her diet—or her running schedule, which she did intend to get back to. She could already feel herself putting on a little weight; she didn't mind so much in that regard, but she didn't want to get too far away from her routine.

"So, my parents told me last night that they want to help me buy a car—which, by the way, is another reason why Europe would be hard for me this summer—I need to put all my extra cash toward it too."

"Oh yeah? That's cool. What are you gonna get?"

Like those of so many of their classmates, Thomas's parents were wealthy. Many of the kids at their school drove BMWs or expensive SUVs. Thomas had had his own BMW since he'd turned sixteen and got his driver's license.

"Oh, you know. Just something practical—small, good on gas mileage so that I can drive it to and from school when I wanna come home."

"Okay, and?"

"And what?"

"Are you planning to come home a lot?"

"No. I don't think so anyway. No more than the school holidays and the occasional long weekend, I suppose. But..."

Thomas looked at her, neither of them speaking for several seconds.

"But what?"

"I dunno. I just think it's gonna be hard on my mom when I leave."

"I'm sure it will be."

Thomas thought that Isabella worried about her parents way too much. He didn't understand it, and he was forever trying to get her to understand how "normal" parent/kid relationships worked. But Thomas wasn't an only child. His parents had other kids to think about, where Isabella's parents had only ever focused on her. He couldn't understand what that kind of pressure felt like.

"I think it will be good for them, though. Don't you? For my parents, I mean. Having me away. Especially my mother, I think."

"Probably."

Thomas was studying her and it looked like he wanted to say more.

"What? Something on your mind about all that?" She smiled, encouraging him to go on.

"Yeah. I was just going to say—speaking of your mother—have you given any more thought to talking to her about your birth mom?"

There it was. That racing of her heart. Even the thought of it made her feel anxious.

"Yeah. I'm just waiting for the right time, I guess."

"How will you know when it's the right time?"

She looked at him across the table, smiling at her slightly as he finished chewing a mouthful of French fries.

"Good point. I'm not sure. I guess I just have to get up the courage. It's not easy, Thomas. I mean, I know you think I need to do a better job of communicating with my parents, but it's a hard thing to bring up. I don't want to hurt them, and it does feel hurtful."

"I know it's not easy. I just think it's something that you deserve. Surely your parents have thought about the fact that you might want to know about your adoption—about your birth mother—at some point. I'm sure they won't be surprised. That's all I'm saying. I don't think you give them enough credit sometimes to be able to handle stuff. It's like you feel this need to protect them and—and it should really be the other way around, Iz."

Isabella nodded, trying to think of how to change the subject because thinking about it was making her feel uncomfortable.

"So, what time are you picking me up tonight for your big celebration dinner?"

Isabella loved hanging out with Thomas's family. His parents were so relaxed and cool compared to her own. Sometimes she wondered what it would be like to have parents like that. They hadn't been bothered at all when Thomas came up with the idea of deferring his college enrollment for a year to travel. If fact, the trip had become their graduation gift to him.

One time when she was over, she saw his parents smoking a joint in the backyard after they thought everyone had left for the evening. Thomas had laughed about it when she told him, saying that they thought they were so sneaky all the time, but he and his brothers knew that they smoked one every weekend.

"Pick you up around seven?"

Isabella nodded. "Sounds good. The usual?"

She suspected that they'd be going to the fun Japanese-style place where they sat around watching the chef do fun tricks with his knives and their pieces of shrimp. She loved going there almost as much as she loved eating at Angelica's.

"Yep, the usual alright. Come hungry."

They both laughed as they finished the last of their fries and Cokes.

FIVE

Isabella took the piece of paper that Ms. Carlson was handing her as she made her way to take a seat in the small office. She'd been thinking about her last meeting all week and had decided that she was going to ask her if there was any way that the counselor would consider meeting with her over the summer. She wasn't used to asking for help when it came to her anxiety and emotional issues, but now that she had found some, she was reluctant to let it go.

"What's this?"

"Read it."

Ms. Carlson had a huge smile on her face as she brought two bottles of water over from the small fridge in the corner of the room.

Isabella read the single sheet of paper in her hand.

"Wait. What? I won?"

It was a letter about the short story contest she'd entered.

"You did, Isabella. You won first place in the whole country. It's really pretty fantastic, you know."

Isabella felt herself grinning. "Wow. I don't know what to say. I'm so surprised."

"I spoke with Mr. Reyes and he says that you're the first

student from here to have ever won, or to even place in the top ten. He's quite pleased with himself for recognizing your talent."

Mr. Reyes had been one of her favorite teachers in high school. She'd loved everything about his class and had learned a lot from him, not only to do with her writing, but her confidence with her writing as well. When he'd approached her about the contest, she'd entered because he'd seemed so enthusiastic about it. She had never even considered she might have a shot of winning.

"Wow, it says here that I've won five thousand dollars. Is that true?"

The trip to Europe falling into her lap? Or more likely, money toward her car so her parents could get some of their travel fund back.

Ms. Carlson nodded. "Yes, you'll be getting a check in the mail within a few days. I'm very proud of you, Isabella. I hope you realize what a big deal this is—how good you are."

Isabella smiled in response. Ms. Carlson had been so supportive of her.

She did know that she was a good writer. Well, she hadn't known for sure, but this past year she'd gotten a lot of feedback from Mr. Reyes and a few other people in her life, including Ms. Carlson.

Thomas thought she was a good writer too, and he used to always give her grief about her aspirations to become a lawyer instead of doing something with her writing. But Isabella didn't even know what "doing something with her writing" looked like. It was so much more vague than the path to becoming a lawyer, and Isabella didn't really deal well with "vague."

Isabella settled back into the chair.

"Thank you—for the news and for all your support. Really. It means a lot to me. I'm not sure I would have survived this past year without your help."

"You're welcome. It's been my pleasure. In fact, I wanted to mention to you that I'm happy to get together once in awhile over the summer if you think that's something that would be helpful to you."

"Yes!"

They both laughed as Isabella continued.

"I mean, I'd love that. I've been thinking a lot about our weekly meetings ending and I was going to ask you the same thing, actually. I'm doing so much better, but I'm kinda anticipating that things could get a little tough as it gets nearer my time to head to school."

"Well, that will work out well then. We can schedule something before you leave here today."

"Great."

"By the way, I really enjoyed your speech. Were you happy with it?"

"Yes..."

"Do I sense a 'but' there?"

"No. I mean, I didn't forget anything and I think it came across well. I know it sure feels good to have it over with." She laughed, knowing that Ms. Carlson knew full well the extent of the anxiety she'd been feeling over delivering the speech.

"Have you been doing the journaling exercises?"

"I have, yes." Isabella laughed. "You've inspired me to take my journaling to a whole new level. It has really helped me to write down my feelings, as you've taught me—to become more present with myself. I think I'm making some good progress anyway. Maybe one day, I'll be slightly less of a freak."

She meant it more as a joke, but even as the words left her mouth, she knew it wasn't funny. But she did feel like a freak at times, so unlike most of her peers who didn't have a care in the world. She felt tears stinging behind her eyelids and it made her angry that she was so emotional all of a sudden.

"Isabella, is that what you really think?"

Ms. Carlson's voice was quiet, and she slid a box of tissues across the coffee table in front of where Isabella sat.

"No. At least not most of the time. I just wish that I didn't worry so much about things. I wish I trusted myself more."

"What do you mean? What don't you feel like you trust yourself about?"

"I used to—trust myself in regards to the decisions I've been making. But I realize more and more that I've been looking at everything through the eyes of my parents—with only thoughts about what they think and what will make them happy."

"And why do you think that is? That you have such a drive to please your parents?"

"I'm sure it has something to do with my being adopted. I guess I've just always felt that I needed to overcompensate in some way—so that they'd not be sorry that they'd chosen me or something."

Isabella laughed because she knew it sounded absurd when she said it out loud and it wasn't exactly what she meant—what she felt. She knew that her parents loved her and that they'd never regret adopting her, no matter what she did or didn't do. They'd both be horrified to hear her say such a thing. She was sure of that.

"Isabella, are you questioning your decisions about Harvard?"

"Oh, no. Not at all. That's not what I mean."

Ms. Carlson, probably more than anyone, had seen how shocked Isabella had been when she'd received the scholarship to the college of her dreams. She'd be crazy not to accept it, period. There was never a question about her going or not.

"Okay, so what do you mean?"

"I guess I've just been more aware lately about what others are doing and the excitement they're feeling—like Thomas, for example, who couldn't be more excited about his upcoming travel plans. I just feel like something is missing for me. I can't quite put my finger on it, but do you think it's normal that I'd have doubts?"

Ms. Carlson was smiling at her. "Do I think that it's normal for an eighteen-year-old girl who's just graduated from high school to not know exactly what her future is going to look like?"

26

"Say no more. Point taken." Isabella laughed. "I dunno. I guess it just feels odd to me because I've always known that I was going to be a lawyer. It's all I've ever talked about with my parents—it's everything that we've"—she caught herself—"that *I've* been working toward."

"But is that what *you* want, Isabella? To be a lawyer?"

Isabella reached for another tissue to wipe at the new tears that had started.

"I think so. I'm not sure what else I would do."

"Well, you know what?"

"What?"

"You don't have to know exactly what you want to do right now. You're so young, and you have a lot of time and experiences ahead of you. Maybe you need to give yourself a little break, Isabella."

She nodded her head because somewhere deep down she knew that Ms. Carlson's words rang true with her. She did need to give herself a break and maybe not take things quite so seriously. Maybe that was what she should spend the next few weeks working on—learning how to relax a little bit. And she could enjoy a few weeks with Thomas before she got busy with the internship. He'd like that. And she could write. Even the idea of that made her smile.

She turned her attention back to Ms. Carlson. "Yes, I think you're right. I think I just need to clear my head. With no tests, track meets, or speeches, maybe I can actually enjoy the start to the summer."

"I like that idea. Perfect. So, just don't go finding things to worry about, okay?"

Isabella laughed. She liked their teasing banter. She trusted Ms. Carlson—probably more than she trusted anyone in her life right now—other than Thomas, of course.

They agreed that Isabella would contact Ms. Carlson when she wanted to set up a next meeting and that they could do so at one of the local coffee shops, now that school was out for the summer.

Isabella left the meeting feeling a sense of lightness that she'd not felt for a very long time. She knew that it was normal for girls her age to question themselves—to question who they were in the world. But she also suspected that it might be a common thread among those who were adopted to have even more challenges about this topic. Who could blame her for feeling like she didn't really know herself at all sometimes?

Not knowing her future was really only one half of the puzzle for Isabella. Deep down, she knew that she had a need to know her past—where she came from. If she thought about it for long at all, she felt that it was the key to the uneasiness that she felt so often— this feeling of not quite belonging, of not quite knowing her place in the world.

Maybe during these next few weeks, she'd actually muster up the courage to talk to her parents again about the adoption. She knew that it was possible that they didn't have any real useful information for her, but she also knew that at eighteen, there were some options available to her now for trying to find some of those answers herself. She only really wanted their blessing with it all— that was the best she'd hope for anyway.

SIX

A few days had passed since Isabella had found out that she'd won the fiction contest and still she'd not told her parents. Thomas was right in that it was slightly insane. She should be proud and they should be proud. Why did she think that they wouldn't be?

She walked downstairs to find her mother behind the desk in her office.

"Hi, Mom."

"Hi, sweetie, what's up?" she said, barely glancing away from her computer.

"Not much. Where's Dad?"

"I don't know. He said something about needing to run some errands." Her mom stopped typing to look over at Isabella as she nestled down in her favorite chair in the corner of the small room. She had memories of sitting there with her coloring book as a child "doing work" while her mother sat at the desk doing her own work.

"Is everything okay? Something you want to talk to us about?"

Isabella nodded. "Yeah, I have some good news, I guess."

Her mom got up and walked over to sit in the chair opposite her daughter.

"I like good news." She smiled, teasing her. "Does it have anything to do with Harvard?"

Isabella shook her head. "No. Not really."

"Well, spill it. Come on. Don't keep me in suspense."

Isabella held up the typewritten papers she held in her hand— five pieces of paper, held together by a paper clip, that comprised the short story that had won her a national honor and five thousand dollars.

"I won a contest—for my writing. It's a short story." She couldn't help but grin as she handed the pages to her mother. "You can read it if you like."

Please love it.

Her mother took the pages from her. "Honey, that's great. Why didn't you tell us that you'd entered something? What did you win?"

Isabella felt her face grow warm and she wasn't sure why she was feeling embarrassed.

"I won first place, actually. And it was a national contest."

She should be proud, and she *was* proud of it. It was kind of amazing to have her writing validated in this way—just because it was something that she loved.

"And I won five thousand dollars."

"Really, Isabella? How wonderful."

She watched her mother walk back across the room to seat herself behind her desk, where she reached for the glasses that Isabella knew she preferred to use whenever she was reading something.

Isabella waited for her to finish, trying to distract herself with her phone and the text conversation she had going with Thomas.

Mom's reading my short story now.

Good. About time. She'll love it.

I dunno. Hope so. She might think it's silly.

Iz. Stop it. You're brilliant!

Don't leave me. I need you. lol

Come to Europe with me. You know you want to! ;)
Meet you in an hour for lunch?
Sounds good. See ya!

She played with her phone for a few more minutes, not really paying attention to anything except her mother's face as she watched her read the story. She couldn't be sure, but she thought she'd seen some sort of reaction. Maybe she'd just reached the part that had made Isabella cry just a little when she wrote it. Many of her stories lately had been more intense, and this one was not an exception.

After what seemed like way longer than the amount of time it would normally take her mother to read such a short piece, Isabella watched her put the papers down on her desk and rub her hands over her eyes before she looked over at her.

"Isabella, I can't believe that you wrote that. Honey, it is really a beautiful, moving story." Her mother walked back over to where Isabella still sat in her favorite chair to lean down and give her a big hug.

"Did you really like it? I mean, you wouldn't lie to me—to spare my feelings or anything?"

"Not at all. Well, I wouldn't tell you that I thought it stunk or anything, but obviously you already know that it doesn't stink at all." Her mother was teasing her, something that didn't happen too often these days—something that Isabella loved.

They both looked at one another when they heard the front door opening.

"Honey?" her mom called out.

"Darling?" Her dad poked his head in the door ten seconds later.

They all laughed, and Isabella thought how great it was that her parents seemed to still be in love after all these years—no one could ever say that she'd not had good role models for what marriage should look like.

She admired her parent's relationship. It wasn't that they

31

didn't argue at all—she'd definitely witnessed her share of arguments over the years—but they always made up minutes later, it seemed, as if they each couldn't bear the thought of the other feeling anything but good about their love.

Mostly, she loved the way that they teased one another.

"Honey, come here. Isabella has some news for you—and something for you to read."

Her mom was grinning, and it was making Isabella feel better than she'd felt about their relationship in a long time. Something about it felt more real to her—that's what she'd been wanting.

Her father was looking from her mother to Isabella while taking the short story that was being handed to him.

"What's this? Go on, then. Tell me what's up that has both of you looking like you've just discovered something amazing."

"Well, I have, actually—and that's this story that our daughter finally shared with me. Go on, tell him, Izzy."

"Mom—the name." But Isabella smiled as she said it. She didn't mind as much in this moment. It felt somehow right for her mom to be calling her by her childhood nickname.

She turned her attention to her father. "So I wrote this short story for a contest. Mr. Reyes encouraged me to enter and—well, I won, actually."

"It was a national contest and Isabella won first place," her mother chimed in.

"And five thousand dollars, believe it or not, which got me to thinking—" She looked over at her dad. "Go ahead and read it first. If you want to, I mean."

"I do want to. I'm going to."

Isabella busied herself again with her phone while her mother went back over to her desk. Her dad finished reading quickly and she could feel his eyes on her while she typed a quick message to Thomas.

"That's really great, Izzy. I'm proud of you, kiddo. Where did you learn to write like that?" He was teasing her, but it wasn't a thought that she'd not had before herself. Neither of her parents was particularly fond of writing so it wasn't something that they'd necessarily encouraged, although they were all avid readers.

"Mr. Reyes, I guess." Isabella laughed. It wasn't exactly true, but he had helped her to grow as a writer this past year. She was really grateful for that.

Her father came over to where Isabella sat and reached his hands toward her so that she'd take them with her own.

"Come here and let me hug you."

Isabella obliged, letting her father pull her up from the chair and take her into his arms for a big bear hug.

"You're gonna be amazing at Harvard, Isabella."

She could see her mom looking over at them from across the room, nodding her head and smiling.

"Your mother and I are so proud of you."

"Yes, we are," her mom called out.

Her father squeezed her one last time and then headed out the door of the office.

Isabella walked over to stand next to her mom, feeling genuinely more content than she'd felt in a very long time.

"Thanks, Mom."

Her mother had a funny look on her face as she turned toward her from behind her desk.

"For what, honey?"

"I dunno. Just for listening to me—for being happy for me."

"Of course I'm happy for you. Your dad and I want nothing more than for you to be happy."

She paused for a moment and Isabella almost looked away because of the intensity that she saw in her mom's eyes. She wasn't sure that it was something that she'd seen there before, and it made her slightly uncomfortable.

"Izzy—Isabella, you do know that, don't you?"

Isabella nodded.

I should talk to her now—really talk to her.

She felt her heart beating faster. "Yeah, I do, Mom."

And then the moment passed as her mom got up from her desk.

"Iz, would you please fix that thing in my e-mail program—what you were telling me about the other day. I can't seem to find the setting."

Isabella's mom was pretty hopeless when it came to anything technical. She was always asking Isabella to look at one thing or another on her computer—which Isabella could normally sort in about two minutes.

"Sure, I'll look at it right now."

"I'll be right back. I'm just going to grab something to eat. Do you want a snack?"

"No, thanks. I'm meeting Thomas in a little while for lunch."

Her mom left the room and Isabella situated herself in front of the computer, feeling pleased with herself for being able to help her mom out.

SEVEN

It took Isabella all of about three minutes to sort out the e-mail issue for her mom. Feeling quite satisfied with herself, she hit the button to get back to the home screen of the program as she got up from the seat—except she must have accidentally hit something else, because now the entire screen was filled with an e-mail. She was sitting back down to close out the e-mail and get her mom's program back to normal when something in the e-mail caught her eye.

She read the first sentence and brought her hands to her mouth to keep from screaming out as her eyes quickly scanned the page, her heart feeling like it was going to beat right out of her chest.

Dear Mr. and Mrs. Dawson,

My name is Douglas Jackson and I'm contacting you on behalf of Arianna Sinclair, the birth mother of a little girl that I believe is your daughter.

I don't mean to cause any problems or angst within your family. I'm writing with the tragic news of Arianna's passing and to let you know that she has left a sizable inheritance in the form of a trust fund to your daughter.

It was not Arianna's intention to cause any grief to your family. Please know this. I only promised her that I would do my best to honor her wishes as they relate to her biological daughter.

Please contact me at the number below so that we can discuss the trust fund and any questions you might have.

Sincerely,
Douglas Jackson

She reread the e-mail a second time and then a third.

She couldn't think—couldn't move. She looked at the date of the e-mail as it all suddenly registered. Her mother had received this e-mail years ago—eleven years ago.

Isabella's birth mother had been dead for eleven years.

Her sobs were sudden and furious. She put her head down into her hands, her body shaking, tears streaming down her face as the full knowledge of what she'd just read hit her.

She would never know her birth mother.

"Did you fix it, Isa—"

Her mother rushed over to where Isabella sat behind the desk sobbing uncontrollably into her hands.

"Izzy, what is it? Honey, what's wrong?"

Isabella felt her mom's hand, trying to push her hair aside from her face. She reached her hand up to push the hand away, filled with a rage that shocked her.

"How could you?"

The question hung in the air, begging for an answer that would never satisfy the enraged girl—not in this moment, anyway.

Isabella looked at her mother standing in front of her, her face now pale as her eyes darted from the computer screen to her daughter's face—a look of sheer terror as she realized what Isabella had seen.

"Oh, honey. God, I'm so sorry. Isabella, let me talk to you." She reached out again to touch Isabella on the shoulder.

Isabella rose to her feet, brushing the tears away with her hand, glaring at her mother as she walked past her toward the door. She didn't want to talk to her mother. She didn't even want to look at her mother. She turned from just the other side of the door to see her mother crumpled on the floor, seemingly overtaken with her own grief about a daughter who hated her in that moment.

For one second, she thought about going to her.

Then Isabella turned and walked away.

She couldn't get out of the house fast enough. She'd bolted up the stairs to her bedroom to quickly throw on her running clothes and shoes. She grabbed her keys, phone, and earbuds all in one swoop from the top of her dresser, and was back downstairs and out the front door in all of three minutes. It was just long enough for her mother to call her dad back into the office. She tried to block out everything, but when she'd come back downstairs she'd seen him kneeling by her mother on the floor. And right before she slammed the door, she heard him call out her name.

She set off at a good pace right away, wishing she'd thought to bring some tissues with her, because it wasn't going to be long before that ugly cry overtook her—it was a rare occurrence for Isabella, but when she did have a good cry, it was often during a run. It seemed to be an excellent outlet for letting out emotions. Ms. Carlson had told her that too, when they'd talked about possible coping methods for Isabella's anxiety.

It was just a matter of moments before she was wiping tears and snot across the arm of her t-shirt. She didn't care. Not really.

She didn't care about anything right now except for the fact that her real mother was dead. Oh, she knew better than to refer to Arianna as her "real mother"; it wasn't politically correct, and all of the experts would call the woman back at the house—the woman who had kept the truth from her for so many years—her real mother. But Isabella was the most angry that she'd ever been at her mother—and the most hurt. For once she wasn't considering her mother's feelings at all. This wasn't about her mother. This was about Isabella and what had been taken from her all those years ago.

She ran a few more blocks to the edge of the park, where she liked to stretch or sit and write in her journal sometimes. Everything had been so busy lately that it had been a while since she'd done either of those things. Now she almost wished that she had thought to bring her journal. Even though her mixed-up crazy feelings seemed more than justified in this instance, her mind automatically went to Ms. Carlson and what she'd have Isabella do right now to cope with everything.

Isabella had already had to throw up once, off into the bushes by the side of the path she'd been running on—that had happened almost as soon as she'd left her front door. It was all those anxious knots in her stomach. Now she tried to remember some breathing exercises, and her tears lessened and her mind went a little numb.

Thomas! She'd forgotten all about their lunch meeting. She looked at the time on her phone as she pulled his number up, realizing that she was fifteen minutes late—also finally seeing the numerous missed texts that had been coming in during the past few minutes.

"Hey, where are you? It's not like you to stand me up."

Isabella burst into tears.

"Hey, Iz—what's wrong?"

Thomas sounded instantly worried, and Isabella loved him for it. She took a deep breath in through her nose, willing herself to speak.

"Isabella? You're starting to scare me a little bit. Where are you? Are you okay?"

"Sorry. Yeah, I'm okay. No, I'm not okay." She started crying into the phone. "I'm in the park. Can you come here, please?"

"Yes, of course. Stay put. I'll be there in five minutes."

She clicked off the phone and allowed herself to cry.

EIGHT

Thomas sat on the bench next to her and hugged her close. Isabella had thought she was done crying, but now her tears came again, almost as steady as the first time she'd cried that day.

"Iz, what's going on? Why are you sitting here crying?"

She lifted her head up off his chest to sit back on the bench and look at him. She swiped her hand across her face and willed the tears to stop for long enough so that she could tell Thomas everything that she'd found out—everything that had just rocked her world to its core.

After she'd told him, they sat quietly, her hand in his as he squeezed it gently. Thomas was very steady and somber next to her, something that Isabella wasn't used to seeing with her carefree best friend who was always trying to make her laugh. But Thomas knew that this wasn't a time for laughter. Isabella felt that sitting next to him after she'd told him everything.

"God, Iz. I'm really sorry."

She looked over at him as new tears started. "What am I supposed to do with this information? I mean it's too late now."

Thomas reached up to put his hand on her back, rubbing it in small circles. Isabella almost laughed despite the seriousness of the moment because it was so unlike Thomas to be so gentle.

Well, that wasn't entirely true. Thomas was always very sweet with her and had been very protective over the years. He really was like the big brother that Isabella had never had. She did smile, because in the moment, she appreciated their friendship so much. What would she do without him?

"What is it too late for? I mean, I kinda understand what you're saying—to read that about your mother must have been so shocking for you. But what are you thinking when you're saying that it's too late?"

"I can never have the chance to meet my mother—my birth mother." She felt slightly irritated for having to explain herself, but she was aware enough to start to understand where Thomas was going with the questions.

"Right. I understand that. But is that why you're so angry with your mom—with your parents?"

Isabella thought about the question for a few seconds. She definitely was feeling anger toward her parents—that much was sure.

"Well, don't you think that they should have told me this information? I mean, okay, I do understand that I was only a kid when they found out, but after all this time?"

"But would that have changed anything? I guess I can kinda see your parents' point in not volunteering it."

"Right. For sure, when I was seven, but what about later? It's not as if the topic came up often, but I know there were moments —small conversations and questions that I'd asked. They should've told me, so I—so I—"

Isabella looked at Thomas and wasn't sure how to continue with what she was saying.

"So that you wouldn't have the hope," Thomas finished for her and then pulled her to his chest again as Isabella cried.

She leaned her head back to look at him. "Exactly. And I did have hope. I really did, Thomas. That one day I'd meet my birth mother and all of these missing pieces of who I am would come together like a puzzle—that maybe she'd think I was pretty amazing just as I am—without Harvard, without any of that. Maybe she'd just think I was great because I was like her in some way. I guess I thought that by some small miracle, I'd meet her one day and we'd be friends. But now that's never gonna happen—I can't believe I'm never gonna have that chance."

Thomas hugged her to him. "I know. That really sucks. I'm so sorry, Izzy."

They sat on the bench for several minutes in silence, Isabella trying to get her head around the letter and all of the questions that were now darting into her mind. She did have questions. She had a lot of questions.

Finally she sat back, feeling something shift inside her just a bit.

"I should contact him. I mean, why wouldn't I? This guy Douglas. I assume that he knew my mother. Of course he did."

"True, but I think you do need to speak to your parents first. Iz, they might have some answers for you. Did that e-mail have a reply from your mom?"

Isabella thought for a moment. She'd been so taken aback by the email, had she even noticed if there was a reply? She didn't think so, but now she couldn't be sure. And the number had been there at the end. Surely her mother would have responded to an e-mail like that in some way. Wouldn't she? And what about the trust fund? What the heck was that all about?

She suddenly realized that she hadn't mentioned that part of it to Thomas.

"Oh, and I didn't tell you. In the letter, this guy—Douglas—said that there was a trust fund for me too."

Thomas arched one of his eyebrows and Isabella laughed lightly at the look on his face. This was the silly Thomas that she knew and loved.

"Now, that's very interesting, isn't it?"

Isabella nodded. "It is. I mean, I'm not imagining it could be a lot of money or anything. I think Arianna—my mother—would have been very young at that time. I don't really know for sure because of everything I've *not* talked about with my parents, but I assume she was young when she had me, anyway."

Thomas was nodding, but he looked thoughtful. "I dunno. I mean, usually a trust fund isn't a small deal. I mean, most people wouldn't go through the trouble of that unless there was something substantial to go in it."

Isabella thought about it for a few seconds. "Well, maybe it's different because she didn't know me. I mean maybe it was more about her connecting with me in some way." Isabella felt her heart jump just a bit with the thought of that. To Isabella, the thought of her birth mother wanting that connection to her was beyond anything that she'd feel about inheriting some sum of money.

Thomas squeezed her hand. "Well, then I guess you should probably start by having a conversation with your parents." He winked at her and Isabella knew that he was right.

It was finally time to get the answers to questions that she'd had all her life.

NINE

Isabella sat on the edge of the bed, her throat sore after having just thrown up in her bathroom. Her darn nervous stomach. When was it ever going to get any better? She didn't want to be that girl at Harvard, freaking out over every test or important project. She'd tried to calm her nerves by writing in her journal, but it was only a jumbled mess. She tucked these thoughts away and tried to focus on her breathing.

She knew that her parents would be downstairs in the living room, fighting their own nerves right now. She'd gone back to Thomas's house after they'd finished talking in the park. She hadn't been ready to confront her parents just yet, but Thomas had made her send a quick text to her mom telling her that she was okay and would be home later.

Her mother had tried to phone her several times, but she seemed to be giving her some space once Isabella had sent the text. Hours later she'd arrived back home to find her parents visibly upset and seemingly frantic to speak with her. Isabella had asked for fifteen minutes to herself and told them that when she came downstairs to talk, she expected answers from them—answers to each and every question that Isabella was going to have.

It was the first time that Isabella had truly felt like the adult she now was. She owed it to herself, her parents, and their relationship to have an honest conversation—to not hold back anything that she was feeling—to not worry about only her parents' feelings for once in her life. At least, she'd try not to.

Now, if she could only stop throwing up due to it all.

Her phone dinged and she picked it up to see a text from Thomas.

Have you talked to them yet?

Not yet. In 10 min. I'm SO nervous.

Don't be nervous. I think everything's going to be fine. Hard, but fine, Iz.

Thank you. And for today. It really helped having you to talk to. xo

Of course. That's what friends are for, silly. Go get em. Be honest. Call me later. xo

Isabella clicked off the phone and then did manage to write the quick exercise in her journal.

Big scary thing: the most honest conversation she'd had thus far with her parents.

Worst case scenario: hmm...she feared some answers that

would make her feel worse than she already did. But what could those possibly even be? She already knew that her birth mom was gone. That was pretty darn bad.

How likely was the worse case scenario and could she die as a result? Not likely; she couldn't imagine feeling worse, but she guessed that there were things her parents could say that could make their relationship go in a bad direction. That would be pretty bad actually. No matter how angry Isabella was feeling now, she had an intense amount of love and respect for her parents—even if these feelings were twisted by feelings of weird guilt at times. And no, probably no one was going to die as a result of anything that was said.

Best case scenario: She'd find out information about her birth mother—a young woman called Arianna. And so maybe she'd be able to finally fill in some of the missing pieces that she'd been feeling about herself for the past few years.

She closed her journal and took a deep breath. Yes, she was going to make this conversation worth every bit of anxiety she'd been feeling.

Isabella sat on a chair across from where her parents sat on the sofa together, holding hands and looking every bit as apprehensive as Isabella felt. They'd both come to her right away when she finally came down the steps a few minutes ago. She'd let them hug her, but for now at least, there was a wall up between them. Her parents had put that wall there—and Isabella felt that only complete honestly from them now would bring it down.

Her mother began. "I just want to first of all say that I'm so sorry for the way you found out about Arianna—about your birth mother."

Isabella could sense how difficult it was for her mother to even use the words "birth mother." Even though Arianna wasn't alive,

Isabella could see something that looked like fear on her mother's face. What was she afraid of?

She nodded and waited for her mother to continue.

"Isabella, it's not that we were never planning to tell you. It just never seemed like the right time, and you've not asked any questions for so long. We just—we didn't know the right way to handle it, I guess."

Her father's arm went around her mother, pulling her nearer to him just a bit.

A united front was what they were. Under normal circumstances, Isabella would appreciate that about her parents, but at the moment, it made her angry—like it was them against her. Even as she had the thought, she knew it wasn't exactly true, though. They might be united as a couple but they were never against her. She did know that deep down.

"Isabella"—it was her father speaking to her now—"we'll tell you everything we know, but we want to warn you that it's not much—not at this point anyway."

Isabella's heart fell at the words. It was more than she'd had a week ago, at any rate.

"Okay. So did you respond to that e-mail that I saw? Did you end up calling Douglas then all those years ago?"

She'd directed the question to her mother, who was nodding her head just as soon as Isabella started talking.

"Yes. Well, not at first, I'll admit. We weren't really sure what to do about it. It was all such a shock. Something that we'd never expected because of the closed adoption. So I didn't respond to the e-mail and if I remember the timing correctly, maybe a week later Douglas left a voice message."

Her parents' eyes met and it was her father who continued then.

"We'd discussed everything at that point and then we did call him back—and we had a few brief conversations after that, but Isabella, we didn't really ask a lot of questions."

Isabella felt the first stinging of tears in her eyes.

"What do you mean? Why? Do you even know how she died?"

"Come sit here with us. Please, Izzy."

Isabella obeyed, coming to sit next to her father on the one end of the sofa.

"We do know how she died, yes. She had an inoperable brain tumor. She was only twenty-two." Her parents' eyes met again as her father reached out his hand to take Isabella's. "You were seven years old when she passed away."

She had been only twenty-two, just four years older than Isabella was now. It was hard to imagine.

Isabella felt oddly a bit disconnected from the information she was hearing. Her real grief was over the fact that she'd not have the opportunity to ever meet her mother; and now that she'd had a little time to process that fact, her mind was full of questions. Questions that she'd hoped her parents would be able to answer for her, but now that seemed to not be the case.

"Okay. So did this Douglas guy say anything else? Who was— who is he anyway?"

Her mother stood up and her father scooted down on the sofa so that she could come around to sit on the other side of Isabella.

"Well, he was her attorney, but I do think he was also her friend. He seemed very emotional about her passing and he was very passionate about getting the message to us."

"He was?"

Her mother reached over to take Isabella's hand. "Yes, he was. We told him that when you were older, we'd be sure that you had the information that you needed and he assured us that we could get in touch with him at any time."

Isabella looked at her mother's face as she continued:

"So I guess that time is now, huh?"

So much of the anger Isabella had been feeling toward her parents dissipated with those simple words. She reached out to hug her mother then.

"I want to know about her but—but, you know that you'll always be my mother"—she looked over at her dad—"you'll always be my parents."

They were all wiping away tears now, even Isabella's father, whom she'd rarely seen shed a tear.

"So, do you want us to call Douglas? We'll help you however you'd like us to be involved—or not, honey. You're eighteen and it's all your call now," her father said.

"And there is something else you should know about," her mother said.

"The trust fund?" Isabella asked and then, seeing their reaction, added, "It was in the e-mail I read also."

"That's right. So, yes. This is a good thing for you to know and a reason why we really were going to tell you about this soon, Isabella. I hope you know that," her mother said. "We didn't get anything specific when we'd talked to Douglas back then. I don't know—I guess we just didn't want anything to be about the money. It wouldn't have gone to you until you turned eighteen anyway, so now is exactly the right time to find out about it."

"It's not really about the money for me either. Mostly I want to find out about her—about Arianna." She turned toward her father. "About contacting Douglas—I think it's something I should do. I'm nervous but I think I'm strong enough to handle it, whatever that looks like."

Her father pulled her in for a big hug. "That's right. You're more than strong enough, Iz."

TEN

Isabella must have read the e-mail twenty times, and still, days after she'd written it, it sat in the draft folder of her e-mail program. She bit her lip as she read through it one last time.

Dear Douglas,

My name is Isabella and I'm writing to you to find out about Arianna—my birth mother. I've only just found out that she has died, which came as a great shock to me. I understand that you had contacted my mother shortly after her death—something that was unknown to me until just a few days ago when by accident I came upon the e-mail pasted below. I know that you said that she'd left something to me and I want you to know that this is not why I am contacting you now.

Amidst my own frustration with my parents and the grief of realizing that I will never know my birth mother, I feel an intense desire to learn more about her—to learn something about the woman who gave birth to me and the circumstances of her life—as well as the circumstances of her death.

I'm not at all sure how to move forward with this but I guess sending this e-mail will be the first step of that.

I hope this finds you well and I'm very sorry to bring up memories of the past if they are painful for you, as I'm not sure what the nature of your relationship was with Arianna. I do appreciate any information you can give me and I hope to hear from you soon.

Sincerely,
  Isabella Dawson

And before she could think about it for a single second more she hit the send button, shut her laptop, and went for a run.

ELEVEN

Isabella felt anxious as she waited for Thomas to arrive at the diner. The entire morning had passed since she'd sent off the e-mail to Douglas. She knew that she needed to be patient, though. If he was still in California, there was a three-hour time difference to account for, but for all she knew, he may have moved somewhere else. She made herself close out the e-mail on her phone to focus on Thomas as she saw him making his way to the booth to join her.

"Hey, sorry, Iz. I got a little held up by the parental units." He leaned down to give her a hug.

"Trouble in paradise?" Isabella laughed. She teased him all the time about how good and weird his relationship with his parents was. Thomas could tell them anything, and they were pretty open themselves.

"Oh, no. We just had to sort out some financial stuff for my trip—all good stuff, really." He winked. "Good ol' Dad is taking care of everything via his travel agent from work."

Thomas's dad was the president of a big tech firm and he seemed to enjoy a lot of perks that came with the position, travel being one of them.

"So what does that mean exactly? Are we talking total luxury here instead of the backpacker dream?"

Isabella had teased him about this when he first started planning the trip. Thomas was used to traveling in style. His parents had taken him on some amazing vacations throughout the years, a couple of which Isabella had even been invited to. There was nothing about a budget vacation that was anything near what he'd experienced, ever. But Thomas wasn't pretentious at all—and neither were his parents. He'd laughed when she teased him about it, saying he was leaning toward something in between budget and luxury, but he would take the first class airfare regardless.

Thomas laughed. "No, not luxury. Keeping it middle of the road. Oh, and on that note—you know that you don't have to pay for anything *when* you come visit me."

She laughed because he'd stressed the word "when." Thomas had already offered to treat her to everything—a week's vacation in Europe with him—but he knew how she felt about accepting gifts like that from him or anyone, really. She'd finally relented, saying that if she did go, he could cover the hotel but she still wanted to get her airfare and pay for any other expenses while she was there. But she also knew that all of this was a very big if.

She turned her attention back to Thomas's question. "Thanks. It really is such a generous offer, and I do appreciate it. I hope you know that."

He nodded. "But?"

"But nothing. Nothing has changed really. Okay, that's not true. A lot may have changed. If and when I hear back from Douglas, I'll probably have an idea of what this money Arianna left me was. I'm guessing it might be enough to cover my flight."

Thomas looked over at her and she laughed.

"But I still have the timing issues and, more importantly—to be honest—the fact that I still can't imagine getting on the darn plane."

"We'll have to work on that. I'll come back to get you myself if I have to. To make you feel better on the plane, I mean."

Isabella laughed. "That's sweet of you, but I'm sure you'll be way too busy partying your way across Europe."

"Bite your tongue. I am going for the history and the culture, of course."

"Of course." Isabella laughed.

"So back to Douglas...I'm guessing, since you've not mentioned it, that you haven't heard from him yet?"

"Nope. I'm trying to be patient. I did only send the e-mail a few hours ago. Do you think he'll even get it? I'd be so frustrated at this point, if he wasn't reachable now after all these years."

"But didn't you say that he had e-mailed your mom every once in awhile over the years to stay in contact?"

"Yeah, but it's been a few years now. He did send her an e-mail with a new phone number awhile back though, so obviously he does want her to keep his current contact information. So, that's a good sign, I guess."

"I'd say so." Thomas grinned at her. "So what do you wanna do today? Are we hanging out after lunch?"

"Oh, shoot. Sorry, I can't. I forgot to tell you that I have coffee scheduled with Ms. Carlson—well, at three o'clock, so maybe we could do something after that if you want to?"

"Oh yeah? That's cool."

Thomas really liked Ms. Carlson also—all the kids at school did. She'd helped him with his deferment process for NYU, so the two had gotten to know one another a little better during that time, something that Isabella was happy for since she had talked about him to Ms. Carlson so much.

"Yeah, I just thought it might be nice to catch her up on everything that's happened this last week. I sent her a text this morning and she got right back to me that she was free today, so that's why the short notice—about our hanging out, I mean. Rain check for tomorrow, though?"

"Yeah, tomorrow should work for me. I really have nothing going on other than my mega video game tournaments."

"Well, I'm so relieved that I can manage to pull you away from your computer for a few hours."

"Anything to spend time with my bestie."

They both laughed.

"So, you've hardly talked about Harvard or the internship at all the last few days."

"Oh, and you miss me talking your ear off about school and work, do you?"

"No, not really. It's nice to see a side of you that's not so consumed by school or work. That's all."

"I know. Honestly, I haven't thought about much else ever since I found out about Arianna. It's almost as if I've just stuck a little placeholder in my life until I hear something. I hope it's soon though, because I'm gonna have to get back to thinking about other things soon. I can't let the whole summer go by without being serious about my studies. And I do have the writing class coming up. That starts in a few days. But it's more fun for me than anything really."

"Oh hey, speaking of your writing. You never did tell me what happened the other day when your parents read your short story. I think that was the day that everything happened."

"It was. Funny you should mention that, because I was all set to tell you how great the conversation with my mother had gone. She seemed to really love the short story and both she and my father at least said that they were really proud of me."

Thomas looked like he was studying her while she spoke. "Why do you always say that as if they wouldn't be proud of you, Iz?"

She shrugged. "I don't know how to explain it. I just feel like the writing seems more frivolous. And I know how hard they've worked to set me up for success—for getting me into the right school and everything. I know how much they've given up for me."

She noticed Thomas didn't seem to be fully buying into her explanation. "What?" she asked.

"I don't know. I just wonder how much of that is in your head. Maybe they have no idea how much pressure you feel. You never talk to them about it—not really. Not as it relates to what you think they feel, anyway."

Thomas did have a point. She did feel that she was opening up more to her parents these days and, as rough as it had been, the conversation about Arianna and Isabella's adoption had made her feel a lot closer to her parents. She finally did feel like she could talk to them about things that were bothering her, especially since she now felt really supported by them in her quest to reach out to find out more about her birth mother.

"Thank goodness I have a friend as smart as you," she teased him.

"You mean, as forthright?" Thomas laughed.

"Yeah, that too. I know you've got my back anyway. That's a good thing."

Isabella grinned as she took a big forkful of food. The volume on her phone was off, but she had it sitting right next to her while she ate her lunch. She saw the notification of the e-mail update out of the corner of her eye. She dropped her fork down against the plate, which made Thomas look up at her.

"Thomas, it's a reply—from Douglas."

TWELVE

Isabella quickly scanned the e-mail, feeling the tears coming. Everything about Douglas's response was perfect. Everything about it led her to believe that he'd been thrilled to hear from her.

"Izzy!"

She looked over at Thomas, who was grinning and waiting patiently for her to finish.

"Well?"

She smiled back at him. "You're really not gonna believe any of this. Want me to read it to you?"

"Yes, of course."

"Okay."

Dear Isabella,

How absolutely wonderful to receive your e-mail. I cannot tell you how happy it has made me and a handful of people that will want to know all about you.

I don't want to overwhelm you with too much information before you tell me that you're ready, but the short version is that I received your e-mail while having dinner in Tuscany, Italy yesterday.

Why is this important, you might ask?

Because I am here along with a small group of people who loved your mother, Arianna, including your biological grandparents who own a vineyard here. The timing of your e-mail with our little reunion has been the celebration of the evening and we are all desperate to talk to you when you're ready.

We'd all love the chance to get to know you, Isabella, and to be able to tell you about your mother, who was very dear to each one of us.

We also have the matter of your inheritance to discuss.

Please let me know your phone number and a good time for you to talk, or feel free to phone me any time at the number below if a phone conversation sounds like a good next step to you.

I will look forward to hearing from you soon.

Sincerely,
   Douglas

P.S. Regarding my relationship with Arianna, I was her friend and attorney at the time of her death, but I've known Arianna ever since her parents brought her home from the hospital as an infant. (Her father was my best friend.)

Thomas handed her a napkin from across the table, and Isabella didn't miss his own tears as he quickly brushed them aside. He got up to join her on her side of the booth, putting his arms around her in a big hug as she wept against his shoulder.

Isabella cried for a good few minutes—from the sheer scope of what she'd just learned in that short e-mail. They were tears of joy for everything that she was going to get a chance to know about her mother. She felt confident in that now.

Finally she pulled away from Thomas when she thought that she'd be able to speak.

"Thomas. I have grandparents."

Thomas grinned. "You have grandparents that live in Italy."

Isabella laughed. "Imagine that. I really can't believe it."

Both of her sets of grandparents had passed away when Isabella was a small child, so to think that she might actually have an opportunity to meet her biological grandparents was incredible to her.

"And Douglas seems very kind, doesn't he?"

Thomas nodded and Isabella thought he seemed genuinely so happy for her.

She wrapped her arms around his neck again, giving him a tight squeeze. "Thomas, what do you think this all means? Who do you suppose that little reunion refers to and do you think I'll get a chance to meet them all?"

He was laughing at her. "Well, let me ask you this. Would getting to meet your grandparents be enough to get you on a plane to Italy?"

"Oh." Isabella stopped smiling for a second, then she laughed. "I hadn't honestly thought about that. Do you think they'd come here?"

"No way. If you get invited to go visit your grandparents at their vineyard in Tuscany, I am absolutely not going to let you turn that down."

Isabella laughed at how he'd stressed the part about them owning the vineyard which was pretty darn incredible.

"Okay, well, I guess I'd have to strongly consider that invitation, but let's not get ahead of ourselves here. I think I'll start by e-mailing Douglas back. Not sure about the timing, but I'll see if he can call me tomorrow at some point. I hope I won't be too nervous to speak to him—it kinda sounded like he's still there—at my grandparents'—didn't it? Oh, how weird that I just called them my grandparents." Isabella laughed at herself and her rambling. "I guess I'm a little excited. What about my parents? I should tell them right away, yes?"

Thomas nodded his head. "Yes, I think so. I mean, there's no reason to keep it from them, right?"

"No. I need to be sure that I keep them involved. I don't want them to have any doubts about anything. I'm sure they don't—not like how it would have been if I was actually getting ready to talk to Arianna—but I still feel like I need to reassure them, ya know? That I'm not going anywhere."

"Try not to worry too much about it. Just let it be what it is."

"Gee, thanks for the advice. Did you get that out of a self-help book?"

Thomas quirked his eyebrow. "It's something my dad says to my mom all the time, actually."

They both burst out laughing, and Thomas moved back around to the other side of the booth to finish his lunch.

Isabella picked up her phone. "So I'm gonna e-mail him back right now. I'll just keep it short and see if there's a time that works for them." She sent off a quick reply and then worked to contain her excitement enough so that she could finish her lunch. Before she'd even finished, she saw that she'd heard back from Douglas already.

"He says tomorrow is perfect. They'll call me at two o'clock."

"What is it, Isabella?"

She guessed that the look on her face was reflecting the P.S. that she'd just read.

"He says to think about coming to visit. Here, let me read it to you...'P.S. I know it's so early to say yes to something like this, but please consider coming to Italy for a visit. We can talk about it more tomorrow and of course only do so if and when you feel comfortable, but nothing would make this little crew here happier than to meet you.'"

Isabella knew she probably looked a bit stunned, but nothing about any of this should really shock her, considering the circumstances of everything that had happened.

"Wow. They want to meet me."

"Of course they want to meet you, Iz. The question is, will you do it?"

Isabella was starting to feel a little overwhelmed with everything. She knew that it wasn't what Douglas had intended, but now that the question of her visiting was out there, she was faced with a whole other set of challenges—namely her fear of flying, but also the fact that she did have such little time this summer with her internship starting the next week. How could she possibly work that out?"

Just let it be what it is. She laughed at Thomas's words, apparently still on her mind just when she needed them, and felt slightly less anxious.

"Isabella."

"Yeah?"

"Everything's going to be fine. I promise." Thomas reached over to grab her hand, and she felt thankful that he was there with her now as she sorted through all of her emotions about what had transpired just in the last hour.

"I know. You're right. I need to just take it one step at a time and not get ahead of myself. For now, I'll focus on the call tomorrow. I don't have to decide anything right now. They might not even want to meet me after we talk. Who knows?"

"Well, they're gonna want to meet you. I mean, unless you're planning to do something really freaky on the phone."

"Oh, hush. Don't jinx me." Isabella looked at her phone then, noticing how much time had gone by since they'd sat down. "Oh, shoot. I gotta run to meet Ms. Carlson. Sorry. I didn't mean to monopolize so much of our conversation."

"Yeah, yeah. No problem."

Thomas never got annoyed about such things. He'd listen to

her talk about her feelings all day, if it would help her. He was a good friend like that.

"Thanks for everything. Call you later."

Isabella set off walking in the direction of her meeting at the cafe, so many thoughts filling her mind—thoughts that she couldn't wait to share with Ms. Carlson.

THIRTEEN

Ms. Carlson listened intently while Isabella filled her in on everything that had happened since she'd last seen her.

"Wow, you weren't kidding when you said that a lot has happened."

Isabella nodded. "Crazy, right?"

"So, tell me how you're feeling in general right now? How's your anxiety?"

"I've been feeling pretty good—once I'd gotten through the rough stuff with my parents—but with this last e-mail I just got from Douglas…"

Isabella didn't even know if she could put into words what she was feeling. Everything had happened so fast, and she really hadn't had a lot of time to process any of it.

"What about it? Are you feeling unsure about wanting to talk with him?"

"No, not that at all. I mean, I am a little nervous to think that I'll probably be talking to my grandparents. That's something I never really expected would happen so soon."

"So, what has you feeling anxious about it?"

"Just at the end of Douglas's e-mail to me, he mentioned that I should think about coming to Italy. I guess I'll know more after I talk to him tomorrow, but it sounds like maybe he will be there for a while. I mean the idea of going to Italy—of meeting my grand-parents—is really kind of crazy. But the idea of actually flying there still does terrify me, even though I know I really do need to get over that fear—that it shouldn't keep me from going—and it wouldn't. I'm pretty sure I could overcome that, but I don't know why I'm even talking about this right now because I can't..."

Ms. Carlson reached out to place her hand on Isabella's arm while she stopped talking for a moment to catch her breath.

"You can't what?"

"I can't go this summer. I have my internship starting next week. There's no way that anything is going to happen that fast. Maybe I could go at the end of the summer, but that's when Thomas wanted me to meet him and I'm afraid I'll be too stressed out about school anyway, so—"

"Isabella," Ms. Carlson interrupted. "Let's stop for a minute."

Isabella laughed. She didn't know what she was getting all worked up about. She'd been perfectly fine a few minutes ago. She guessed that it was because she'd grown to be so comfortable here, talking to Ms. Carlson—like she could really be herself with her.

"Okay, sorry. It's just that all of a sudden, everything is hitting me and I realize that none of what I'm talking about has a remote chance of happening—just because of the timing, I mean. Except for the communication, of course. There's no reason why I can't just be content with the e-mails and phone calls for now, right? I'm sure they'd extend another invitation to come visit for later in the year. At least I'd assume that they would."

"Well, let's just hold on for a minute and talk this through."

Isabella sat back in her chair, trying to convince herself to calm down again as she listened to Ms. Carlson.

"Let's talk about choices." She winked at Isabella. "Because you do have some here, you know."

"Okay."

"Firstly, it sounds like maybe you're getting ahead of yourself just a bit. You'll probably have more of an idea after tomorrow's call as to whether you'd even like to go for a visit, right?"

Isabella nodded. She'd been telling herself this too, but it didn't stop her mind from racing ahead to the possibilities.

"Second thing to consider...about your internship. What would happen if you didn't do that? Could you not do it? Do you think you could get them to postpone your start date? So that you could take a few weeks to go to Italy if you decided that's what you wanted?"

Ms. Carlson waited while Isabella considered the questions.

"I feel like I can't say no to the internship. I think my parents would kill me if I didn't do it. It's such a good opportunity, really—for anyone going into law." She let herself just sit with the thought for a moment.

"What's that look? What are you thinking?"

"Well, for one thing when I took the internship, it was about more than just the money; but for sure I needed the money that a summer job would bring me. But now I don't know if that's as much of a concern any more. I have no idea what this sum of money is that Douglas has mentioned—the trust fund from Arianna, from my mother—but he certainly made it sound substantial enough that I'm guessing not working this summer wouldn't hurt too much. So, I guess it could be an option."

"And what about how your parents might feel about that? Do you think you can be okay if they disagree with your decision?"

A week ago Isabella didn't think she would be okay with something like that—not by a long shot—but now, after everything that had happened, after the conversations that she'd had with her parents in the last few days, she felt like maybe it was time for her to start making some decisions without worrying so much about their approval.

She nodded slowly in response to Ms. Carlson's question. "Yes. I think if I could get to a place where I'm comfortable with that as a decision, I'd be okay with it, regardless of what my parents think. Do you think that's selfish of me?"

She wasn't sure why she bothered asking the question, really. She knew what Ms. Carlson's answer was going to be. It was something that they'd talked about in the past—how Isabella needed to start making decisions for herself, without worrying so much about what her parents or other people thought.

"Isabella, I think you're a very smart young woman, fully capable now of making decisions for your life as the young adult that you are. It would be one thing if we were talking about decisions that could harm you or set you going down a wrong direction in life, but that's not the case here. As much as I know you think your parents have this idea of what your ideal future should be, maybe they'd surprise you. Maybe you don't give them enough credit."

Isabella considered Ms. Carlson's words and had to admit to herself that there might be some truth to them. She wasn't sure any more if all of these expectations she'd been heaping on herself over the years were because of her parents or some kind of false assumption that she'd held about what they wanted for her.

She was sure that they wanted her to be successful—to strive for excellence—but maybe her ideas about what that looked like were not the same as what she thought her parent's ideas were. Her mother had said something to her just the other day after reading her short story—right before all the craziness happened—about her and Isabella's father just wanting Isabella to be happy. Did she mean it? What about her writing? Isabella barely let herself have the thought—there were too many other things to think about right now.

She turned her attention back to Ms. Carlson. "Sorry. I guess I'm kind of spacing out a little."

Ms. Carlson laughed. "I don't know if it's so much that you're spacing out or that you just have a lot on your mind, which is completely understandable. I'm really proud of you for how you're handling all this, by the way."

"Thank you." She smiled. "And who knows about my parents? Maybe you're right. I think I won't say anything to them just yet about Italy. There's no reason to until I speak with Douglas. But they don't even know yet that he's replied to my e-mail. It only happened a few hours ago while I was at lunch with Thomas."

Ms. Carlson looked at her watch. "Well then, I'd say it might be a good idea for you to go home and bring them up to speed. I have a feeling that they might be happy for you—now that everything has started. I'm sure that it hasn't been easy for them either —knowing this information about your birth mother all these years."

Isabella nodded her head. Yes. Now that they'd gotten through the worst of it, she did feel that her parents were being honest with her in terms of what they did and didn't know. She'd already forgiven them for keeping the information from her. There would be no moving forward with anything if she kept that hanging over their heads. Nothing was worth that kind of stubbornness, and certainly not the relationship with her parents, who had loved her for her whole life.

Isabella said goodbye, promising Ms. Carlson that she'd let her know how the phone call with Douglas went the next day.

FOURTEEN

Even though Isabella had been watching the clock all day, she jumped when her phone rang promptly at two o'clock. She was in her room sitting on her bed and she knew that her parents would be downstairs waiting when she was finished. When she'd filled them in about Douglas's reply to her e-mail and the scheduled phone conversation, they'd certainly seemed pleased for her. She thought they were handling everything very well and were being quite supportive, now that they all had the same knowledge about Isabella's birth mother. Isabella could imagine that her knowing about her mother's death had probably lifted a burden from them of the secret that they'd been keeping from her.

She suddenly needed to use the restroom for the third time in the past thirty minutes, but there was no time for that. One ring, then two, three...

Just be yourself, Isabella.

"Hello?"

"Isabella?"

The voice was clear and deep and if she had to guess, she could picture the man smiling widely on the other end.

"Douglas?" She laughed and to her own ear it gave away her nervousness. God, she really was nervous.

"Yes. It's so good to hear your voice. You have no idea how much I—how much we—have been waiting for this day."

"I've been really excited too. Ever since I got your e-mail. So, you are in Italy right now?"

"Yes, my wife, Gigi—who's dying to talk to you, by the way—and I are here visiting Lia and Antonio—your grandparents—for a few weeks. They live here in Tuscany." He laughed. "There's so much to say, isn't there, but we want to hear about you. Isabella, do you mind if I put you on speakerphone? It's my wife, Gigi, and your grandparents here with me."

"Sure." She laughed a little bit. "Hello, everyone."

It was quiet on the other end of the line for a few seconds.

"Douglas?"

"Sorry. Both Gigi and Lia are a little emotional right now." He laughed, but Isabella felt tears stinging her own eyes for the impact this phone call was already having on her.

Finally she could hear a woman's voice in her ear, soft and lovely. "Isabella? It's your grandmother." Her voice caught and then a man's voice cut in. "And your grandfather."

'We've waited so long to hear your voice—to see you." It was the woman again.

"You have?"

"Oh, yes. From the moment I learned about you, I couldn't wait to meet you. I couldn't believe that I had a lovely grand-daughter out there somewhere."

Isabella's mind was spinning. She had so many questions—far too many for a first phone call.

"Will you send some pictures? Maybe you can send them to Douglas's e-mail."

"Sure."

And she wanted to see her grandparents—and her mother. She couldn't wait to see what her mother had looked like. For all these years she'd wondered if she looked like her—if she had her mother's eyes, her hair, her coloring.

Her grandmother was talking again. "Isabella, there's someone else here who's waited to talk to you for a very long time. She knew your mother the longest out of all of us. I—I don't know how much you know about your mother's and my relationship, but I think it's all too much to talk about over the phone. But I want to talk to you about everything one day soon. I hope that we can arrange for that."

Isabella was nodding her head, forgetting to speak as she tried to take it all in.

"Isabella, this is Gigi. She took care of your mother for most of her life. Are you there? Oh, I hope we're not overwhelming you too much," her grandmother said.

"No. No, I'm here. I'm just trying to take it all in—hearing all of you speak and the words about my mother. It's all a lot—but it's all good. Please go on."

"Hi. Isabella?"

"Yes. Hi. Gigi, is it?"

"Hi, lovely girl. I just can't believe that I'm talking to you right now and I can't wait to see you." The woman's voice was a bit shaky, like she was trying very hard to keep it together.

"I can't wait to meet you all too." Isabella's voice was quiet, and as she said the words out loud, she knew that it was true. She wanted to meet them as soon as possible. She could tell that already just from the brief words that had been spoken. She could feel so much love for her coming from these people whom she'd never met, yet felt oddly connected to.

"Well, let's see about making that happen, shall we?" It was Gigi's voice still.

"Isabella, it's Antonio. Lia—your grandmother—and I would love to have you come stay with us. Stay as long as you like. We have plenty of room and we'd love the chance to get to know you."

Isabella liked the sound of her grandfather's strong Italian accent. He sounded kind and like someone out of one of the foreign films she'd watched with Thomas.

"Yes, please say you'll come." It was Lia speaking again. "I'm guessing Gigi and Douglas will extend their stay and Jemma's here waiting to meet you. Oh, you probably don't know about Jemma —she's your age, actually. Her mom, Blu, was Arianna's—your mother's—best friend. So they've just left to take care of some things back in California, but she says they'll return the minute they find out that you're coming."

Isabella was laughing on the other end of the line. She loved the excitement that she heard in their voices over meeting her. And she was feeling that same excitement. She wanted to go, but could she be sure that she'd be able to make the trip without having a nervous breakdown?

"I hope we're not overwhelming you." It was Douglas again. "I just want to be sure that you know that we'll take care of the ticket —of everything—so there's no need to worry about any of the expense. Well, we have the matter of your trust also. I think you're going to be quite surprised when you find out what Arianna— what your mother had set up for you. We can talk about that soon at another time, but let's just say that you won't need to be concerning yourself with any worry or thoughts as they relate to your financial situation for a very long time."

"Well, thank you—for making me feel so—I don't know what the right word is—"

"Loved." It was Gigi's voice interrupting her, and Isabella felt tears stinging her eyes instantly. "We've all loved you for a very long time, Isabella. And we loved your mother very much."

"We'd really like the opportunity to, not only get to know you, but also to tell you all about Arianna...and how much she loved you too," said Lia.

Isabella could hear gentle sobbing in the background as she tried to collect her own words before trusting herself to speak.

"I do feel loved. Incredibly so—so thank you for that. And I think I would like to come visit, sooner rather than later, but I do have some things to think about here. Some stuff going on this summer that I might need to move around and—and just a few other things."

She wouldn't dump all of her anxiety and stupid fear of flying on them now. She'd just have to see what kind of headway she could make with it in the next few days, and if she really couldn't muster up the courage to do it—she'd tell them. She wouldn't want them to think for a moment that her not coming had anything to do with not wanting to meet them.

"Douglas?"

"Yes. I'm here."

"Can we talk again in a couple days? I should have an answer by then. I mean, that's assuming you all are serious, I guess, about me coming right away?"

"Oh, yes. We're serious." Douglas laughed. "But you take all the time you need."

"If you can call me at this same time the day after tomorrow, I think that should be enough time. And I do want to make it happen. You all have no idea what this has meant to me, and the idea of finding out about my birth mother..."

It was Isabella's turn to cry quietly into the phone.

"We will, Isabella—make this happen." It was Lia's voice.

"And we love you, bella—so much," said Gigi.

Isabella said goodbye before she burst into the tears that threatened to take over any words that she had yet to speak.

She called me bella. Maybe I am a Bella.

She grinned. And even though she hadn't even met them yet, there was a rightness to it all—meeting these people who loved her mother—and in her heart she knew that she'd love them all too.

FIFTEEN

The slight sound of her feet hitting the pavement created a rhythm that Isabella found relaxing. She'd started running long-distance on the track team during her freshman year of high school, and quite soon after realized that it seemed to have a very calming effect on her when she was feeling particularly stressed out or having a bad day. Today, she wasn't feeling anxious as much as she was trying to make sense of all the swirling thoughts and emotions that she'd been feeling ever since she'd hung up the phone with Douglas and the others.

She felt a quick pang of guilt as she thought about how she'd raced out of the house, stopping in the living room only for a moment to tell her parents that the call had gone great and that she just needed a little time to herself to think about everything. They'd hugged her and seemed fine about it, but now she was feeling like she should have spent more time with them—that she wasn't being fair leaving them in the dark.

She sighed. It was okay for her to think about herself right now. She needed to do that. And her parents would be fine. She needed to keep telling herself that.

She let her thoughts return to the earlier phone conversation, feeling herself smile as she remembered how excited everyone had been to speak to her. There wasn't a question in her mind whether she wanted to meet her grandparents—and Gigi and Douglas and the others that they'd mentioned—it was more of a question of how to work it all out. And the real question being: would be she able to get on the plane?

Isabella rounded the corner of the path that she'd run day after day, for the past four years, setting off for the first of several ten-second sprints that she'd do over the course of her run. Thomas teased her endlessly about being such a creature of habit, and Isabella did think it peculiar at times that the two of them hit it off so well, despite their obvious differences. As much as Isabella craved routine, Thomas was the most spontaneous person that she knew. She smiled when she thought about the fact that he knew—and fully supported—her secret dreams that she'd not told to anyone else. Dreams that would have her living a life as non-routine as anything she could do. Maybe Italy could be the start of that? She let herself have the fleeting thought as she pushed right past it to the logic of what would need to happen in order for her to make this trip to Tuscany.

She'd have to fly—or more specifically, tackle this silly fear that she had of flying. Putting that aside, she'd need to contact the firm that she was doing the internship for. She'd at least find out if there were any possibility of pushing her start date out by a few weeks. That might take care of answering some of the other questions for her, because she doubted that she'd give up the internship—no matter how anxious she was to meet everyone. She still had her future to think about—Harvard to think about.

And then there was the issue of her parents. She was going to assume, based on how they'd been handling everything so far, that they'd be supportive of her desire to make the trip, so she'd try not to let that concern enter into her decision at this stage.

Isabella let her pace slow as she came out of her final sprint, just then spotting Thomas in the distance. She'd texted him to meet her in the park—in their usual spot closer to his house—in a half hour. Thomas was in good shape but he wasn't much of a runner, so often he'd walk with her after she'd had a good run. It was a little ritual they'd started this past track season when Isabella had been keeping to a very rigorous training schedule—a ritual that she was going to miss greatly when she and her best friend parted ways this summer. She couldn't think about that now—how badly she was going to miss having Thomas there every day.

"Hey, speedy." Thomas jogged to meet her on the path, giving her a hug and falling into step beside her as they continued walking back toward where she'd started.

"Hey yourself. Thanks for meeting me."

"You know I can't wait to hear everything. How was the phone call? Spill it."

Isabella recounted the conversation to him and by the end of it, Thomas had stopped, pulling her off the path to sit on a nearby bench. He was grinning at her like a madman.

"What? What's that look for?" She laughed. She never could tell what mischievous thought was going to come out of Thomas's mouth. He was always surprising her in that way and she loved it about him—about their friendship.

He was staring intently at her now, still smiling.

"It's you. Iz, you look the happiest I've seen you—maybe ever. And I must say, given the things that are still up in the air, you seem surprisingly calm about stuff—much calmer than your typical frantic self." He laughed and Isabella punched him lightly in the arm.

"You think so?" She didn't wait for him to answer. "It's funny that you say that, because something about talking to them has made me feel calm—relaxed about it all. Like I don't have to worry about it or anything. I know that if I don't see them this summer, it will happen. I'm sure of that and I think they are too—that they want to meet me as much as I want to meet them."

"Wait. Who are you and what have you done with my best friend?"

Isabella laughed at the mock-serious look on his face. "I know. I'm not sure that I know myself these days."

There was a certain irony to the statement that she took in, even as the words left her lips. Maybe that was exactly what *was* happening—she was finally getting to a place of knowing herself, where she came from, and answers to so many of the questions that she'd had for most of her life.

"So, what's the next step?"

"I was just thinking about that. I need to call about the internship."

"Okay. Do you have the number with you?"

Isabella bit her bottom lip. She did feel a little apprehensive about it. "Yeah, it's in my phone."

"Call them now. Let's find out."

She looked at Thomas and nodded. She might as well get it over with.

"Okay. I'll do it."

She brought the number up on her phone, and within seconds she was speaking with the person in charge of the internship program. She got up to take a few steps away from where Thomas was sitting on the bench because she wanted to sound as professional as possible, and Thomas's listening to her was making her feel slightly nervous.

Isabella finished the call and walked back to where Thomas sat, feeling more confused than ever.

"So what's the verdict? You don't look exactly pleased, so I'm guessing it wasn't as easy as just postponing your start date."

Isabella shook her head. "Nope. Not so easy. They won't do it. If I can't start next week, the number two person on their list for the position will be called. I guess it's only fair. It's a very coveted position, you know."

Thomas winked. "So you've said."

"Yep..."

"But?"

"Well, I guess that's that then. There's always the couple of weeks I have at the end of the summer, I suppose—before school starts. I mean, I don't know how you would feel about that? If I went to Tuscany instead of meeting up with you? Or maybe you'd meet me there?"

"Sure. You know I'd understand that, and I'd say there's a good possibility that I could meet you—but Iz..."

"Yeah?"

"You seem really disappointed."

"I guess I am. I guess I'd gotten my hopes up that somehow this could work and I'd be meeting my grandparents in Italy next week." She laughed. "It's silly really—that I expected things to happen so fast."

"Well, you could just decide not to do it—the internship. I mean, is it really going to make that much of a difference in the big scheme of things? Knowing you, your resume will still look great by the time you're ready to start applying to law school."

It wasn't as if the thought hadn't entered Isabella's mind, but hearing Thomas ask the question somehow brought it all into perspective. Could she just not do it? The idea that she was sitting there considering it shocked her a bit. She'd been so pleased when she'd landed the position. But so much had happened since that day—things that were now more important.

"Well, I should probably wait until I talk to Douglas tomorrow to decide. I mean I guess I do need to have some kind of idea about this trust fund too. I think that it should be enough to cover the summer job, but I guess I really have no idea. If it isn't, I can't just give up the work so easily—not with school coming up shortly after."

Thomas was nodding his head.

"And then there's the issue of flying." She sighed, thinking about it. "Well, I'm not going to let my nerves stop me. I'll just have to get my doctor to prescribe something to knock me out for the length of the flight, I suppose." She laughed, despite how apprehensive the idea of flying still made her.

Thomas reached over to take her hand. "Iz, I promise you that you'll be fine on the plane. I really do think this is a good idea—despite the fact that I'm guessing it would mean that you wouldn't come back to meet up with me in Europe later this summer."

Isabella nodded her head slowly. "Oh, I'm sorry, Thomas. You're probably right about that. But maybe I could meet you somewhere later in the year—during one of my breaks."

He reached over to hug her. "Yeah, I'm sure we could work something else out. I'll be happy for you—for the fact that you'll be meeting your family."

Her family. It was all still so surreal. She felt the twinge of regret for not having that chance to meet her birth mother, but knowing that that was no longer possible, she knew that knowing her grandparents would be the next best thing. And they'd tell her all about her mom. It would be so much more information than she'd ever had.

"Thomas."

She said his name quietly.

"Yes?"

"I think I'm gonna do it." She grinned. "I'm going to go to Italy next week and meet my grandparents."

SIXTEEN

Isabella walked in her front door slightly out of breath after sprinting the last several blocks to her house. She felt lighter for having made the decision. Now she just needed to double-check with Douglas about the trust fund amount, and as she heard her parents' voices coming from the office, she was reminded that she needed to have a talk with them—to tell them about the internship. Her heart beat faster thinking about it. They had been very supportive, but this internship was a very big deal.

She walked through the house to the office and stuck her head in the doorway.

"Hi, guys. What are you doing?"

"Oh, just catching up on some reading," her father said.

"How was your run, sweetie?" her mother asked, crossing the room to sit next to her father on the small sofa.

"It was good." She leaned over to hug each of them before settling into the chair across from the sofa.

"So, I'm sorry for running out of here so fast after my phone call with Douglas. I realize that it was kind of unfair to leave you guy hanging like that."

She noticed her father reaching over to hold her mother's hand as he spoke. "Honey, we understand that this is a lot for you to process. Are we curious as to what Douglas had to say? Yes, of course we are, but we don't want to get in the way of you figuring all of this out. You just need to know that we're here for you—that you have our support."

Her mother was nodding in agreement, and Isabella noticed the tears in her eyes at the same time as she felt her own. She recounted the phone conversation for the second time that day, and like Thomas, her parents seemed genuinely excited for her.

"They certainly sound wonderful," her mother said.

Isabella nodded. "They also invited me to come visit—to come to Italy where Lia and Antonio—to where my grandparents live."

She watched her mother's face carefully.

"Wow. Do you think you'd be comfortable with that, honey?"

"Yes, I do actually. I don't know how to explain it, but it felt pretty comfortable talking to them on the phone. How would you guys feel about that?"

She didn't miss the quick glance between her parents.

"Well, I'd be lying if I said that I felt completely comfortable with you traveling to Italy by yourself to meet up with people who are virtually strangers to you, but I do understand why you would want to go. Is there any way that they'd consider coming here first?"

"No. I mean, maybe they would but I want to go." She looked at them carefully. "I've decided that I'm going to go. I need to talk to Douglas tomorrow to finalize everything, but I think I'm going to go next week." She took a deep breath as she waited for someone to speak.

"Next week? Don't you think that's a little soon?" her mom said.

"Honey, doesn't your internship start next week?" her father asked.

"Yeah, that's the thing. I'm not going to do the internship after all. I haven't officially told them yet but I've decided that my doing this trip is worth missing out on the internship."

She didn't even have to convince herself when she said it out loud. She knew without a doubt that it was what she wanted.

"I don't know, Iz. Are you sure about that? Honey, you worked hard to get that internship. We hate to see you throw away the opportunity," her father said.

"Yeah, I know. It wasn't exactly an easy decision."

"Can't you visit them another time?" her mother said.

Isabella could see the concern on their faces, but she'd figured that they'd have some strong opinions about her plans. She was ready for it—or at least she'd thought she was—but looking at them now she had to remind herself of why she was doing this.

She took a few seconds to collect her words before she answered her mom's question.

"I suppose I could visit them another time, but I don't know how I'm gonna feel right before school starts—and who knows what the actual year is going to be like? I can imagine that I might feel a little stressed with everything."

She was trying to justify her decision, and she reminded herself that she didn't need to do that.

"And—well, the truth is that I don't want to wait. It's important to me, and I can't explain it but I think it's important that I go now."

Her parents seemed to be taking in her words, not exactly looking convinced, but Isabella got the impression that they knew she was serious—that there'd be no convincing her to change her mind. She was resolute when it came to making decisions. Her parents had taught her that.

"Well, it seems as if you've made your mind up then," her father said.

Isabella nodded. "I hope you both understand and will support me in my decision." She looked at her mom, waiting for her response. "It really means a lot to me, you know."

Her mom got up to walk over and hug her.

"Of course we support you. I'd like to think that your father and I raised you to make good decisions, and you've never let us down once. There's no reason for us to think that you're going to do that now. We might question you, but it's only because we care about you and your future. You know that, right Isabella?"

She nodded and hugged her mom back. "Thanks. I think I really needed to hear that from you guys. I'm not going to call about the internship until after I speak to Douglas tomorrow. I do need to have more information about this trust fund that's coming —to make sure that I don't need to worry about the financial aspect of giving up the job. That I wouldn't do. Not with a year away at school right in front of me. I know my best earning potential is going to be over the summers when I'm not enrolled in classes. So it's possible that the whole thing really will be a bust. I just want to be prepared either way."

"Well, it sounds like you've thought this all through." Her father stood up and Isabella took a step to give him a hug.

"I have, Dad. Really. I want you guys to trust me."

"We do, honey. You just let us know how your talk with Douglas goes tomorrow and we'll take if from there." Her dad smiled and hugged her tight.

"I will. Thanks."

And just like that she felt another weight lift from her shoulders.

SEVENTEEN

For the second time that week, Isabella waited anxiously for her phone to ring. For the second time that week, Douglas was right on time with the phone call.

"Hello?"

"Hello, Isabella?"

"Yes. Hi, Douglas." She smiled as she said his name and hoped that he'd be able to tell how pleased she was that they were talking.

"How are you doing?"

"I'm great, thanks. How is everyone there?"

"We're all fine. We've been talking a lot about you—about our phone conversation the other day—and we hope that we didn't overwhelm you." He laughed.

Isabella liked his laugh.

"No, not at all. I've not been able to think of anything else since our conversation. It's very exciting to talk to you all—to get to know you. And I think I have some good news—if Lia and Antonio are still okay with me coming for that visit?"

"Yes, it's all we've been talking about. We'd like the chance to meet you as soon as possible—again, not to overwhelm you, but it really is something we've been wanting for years. I want you to know that." Isabella thought she could hear Gigi in the background. "Can you hear that?"

"Is that Gigi?"

"It is. She's saying that you should come tomorrow."

Isabella laughed lightly. "Well, I'm not so sure about tomorrow, but I have been thinking about next week as a possibility..."

"Really? That's exactly what we were hoping. And we've talked to Blu. She's ready to return any time."

"Blu?" Isabella was a little bit confused by the names being thrown around. She understood about her grandparents and she knew that Gigi had been like a nanny to Arianna—at least she was pretty sure that this was what she got from their earlier conversation. But she still wasn't clear who this Blu person was. And Douglas mentioned her so casually—like she was part of one of their families.

"Sorry. We keep talking to you as if you have an idea who we all are. Blu was a big part of your mother's life. She was her best friend and knew her probably the best of any of us—well, aside from Gigi, I suppose. And Blu's daughter is Jemma. She's your age and staying here with Lia and Antonio right now. Jemma's an artist." Douglas stopped suddenly, laughing. "I'm sorry. There are so many gaps in all this for you. I just want to tell you everything, but of course we have time—lots of time if you'll be coming here next week. How long will you be able to stay, do you think?"

"I like hearing about everyone. Don't apologize for that. It's fun for me and only makes me more excited to meet you all. Okay, so about my coming. I suppose I do need to get some clarity on a few things. I'll let you know upfront that I'd be giving up my internship—my summer job. Honestly, I can't pass up the earnings —Oh, I'm going to Harvard in the fall, so I need the money for some of my living expenses, but I've decided it's okay to not take the job if—" Isabella stopped herself from continuing. "Wow. I'm sorry. Now I'm going on and on." She laughed.

"Did you say you were going to Harvard?"

"Yeah." Isabella felt her face growing warm, which was funny, but at the same time she felt a bit self-conscious. She wasn't one to brag and she didn't normally volunteer information that would paint a certain type of picture of her with strangers.

"Isabella. Honey, that's incredible."

Isabella grinned at Douglas's term of endearment, which for some reason seemed perfectly natural to her even though it was only the second time they'd ever spoken.

"Thank you. I got a full scholarship, actually. Otherwise— well, there's no way that I could have afforded to go there without one. But I—I do work very hard in school, getting good grades and all."

"I guess so. That's quite an accomplishment."

Isabella couldn't explain it, but she liked the idea of Douglas being proud of her. Just the thought of it already made her feel good.

"Thanks. But so anyway—about the job. I guess I—I'm just wondering about this trust fund you've been talking about. Oh, sorry. It feels weird asking about that. Honestly, I hope you all know that it's not about any money—that none of this is about the money for me. But—but it's something that I need to find out about if I really am going to give up this job. That's all."

There were a few seconds of silence on the other end of the line and for a split second, Isabella wondered if she'd made a mistake.

Finally, Douglas was clearing his throat. Isabella waited for him to speak.

"Sorry. Isabella, I swear I get more emotional the older I get. My wife says that I'm the biggest softie she knows. She's made me that way in part, I guess."

Isabella smiled because she heard a sound that could only be Gigi's lips against his cheek.

"So, Arianna had taken great care before she died to set up her will. As her attorney, I helped her with that and I'd helped her father before that. Oh, this is so much to tell you over the phone—

it would be better in person, but I want this to at least make some sense to you. Do you have time now? I think this might take more than a few minutes."

"Yes, of course. Take all the time you need."

Isabella settled back into her chair as she listened while Douglas told her that Arianna had also been adopted—that she'd only met Isabella's grandmother the year that she died and that Arianna and Antonio, her father, had never had the chance to meet. He told her about Arianna's own adoptive parents dying in the plane crash and then he told her about the vast wealth that she'd inherited.

By the time Douglas had gotten to the point of telling Isabella that the amount of money Arianna had left her would be more than what she'd ever need to live on for the rest of her life, Isabella was shattered, tears streaming down her face—beside herself with a crazy mix of emotions. It was all so much to take in, and it only left her more in awe for this woman who'd been her mother—for the care that she'd taken to be sure that Isabella would be more than cared for by this crazy amount of money she'd left her.

"Isabella?" Douglas was speaking quietly in her ear on the other end of the phone line. "Are you still there, honey? I'm so sorry to blurt all of this out to you over the phone. I'm sure it's a lot to take in."

"I'm here." Isabella's voice was quiet also as she struggled to speak through her tears. "I just can't—it's all so much to take in. I had no idea—no idea about any of this. Thank you, Douglas—for sharing all this with me. It's really helping with the puzzle pieces and some of the questions that I've had ever since I found out that Arianna—that my mother had passed away. And the money—just wow. I can't even comprehend what you're telling me about that. I'm sure it will take a while to all sink in, but for now you've given me the answer that satisfies the remaining question I had about leaving this summer job behind. Oh, well, I guess there's one other thing I should tell you..."

Isabella wasn't even sure it was worth mentioning her fear of flying, but what if she really couldn't go through with it—when it came right down to getting on that plane? She took a deep breath in. No. She'd never let that happen. Not any more. Meeting them, hearing about Arianna, and seeing pictures of her mother would make every bit of that flight worth it, no matter how difficult it would be for her.

"What is it, Isabella? I know you don't know me well yet, but you can trust me. I just need for you to know that. Whatever misgivings or questions you might have, we're all here to make this as easy for you as we can. We'll never stop doing that for you, honey. The thing that was the most important to Arianna those last days of her life was a promise we all made to her—that one day we'd find you and tell you about her—that you'd know how much she loved you from the moment you were born."

Isabella felt like she couldn't breathe. She was overwhelmed by everything that she'd just learned—and by the words from this man whom she trusted so completely. She took a few deep breaths, not trusting herself to speak yet.

"Isabella? Are you there? Are you okay?"

"Yes, I'm here. Sorry, I'm trying to pull myself together enough to speak." She laughed lightly, willing the tears to stop so that she could answer Douglas's question. She wanted to be completely honest with him—with all of them. She knew without a doubt that it would be the most important decision she could make as she moved forward with everything.

"It's okay. Take your time."

And she knew everything was going to be okay—more than okay. She took one more big breath in before she spoke.

"So the only other thing—and I should say that it's not going to keep me from coming, so I'm not even sure why I'm telling you this—is that I have this issue with anxiety sometimes. It's something I've really been working on, but I—I've always had this pretty intense fear of flying. I've never flown before actually and, well, it's just something that's making me a little apprehensive. But like I said, I'm not going to let it stop me. I figure I'll get some Valium or something that should help from my doctor and I—"

She stopped to take a breath and could hear what sounded like quiet words between Douglas and someone else on the other end of the phone line.

"Isabella, I have an idea if you're game for it," said Douglas.

"Okay. I'm all ears if you know a special trick that will help me with this flying business." She laughed and waited for him to continue.

"I have to fly to Guatemala—back to the orphanage— tomorrow for a few days and then I could come to you. We can fly together to Italy, so at least you won't be alone on the flight. What do you think?"

"Really? You would do that? And wait—what do you mean by the orphanage?" Isabella laughed. There was so much to learn about these people who had suddenly come into her life; already she found them all incredibly fascinating.

Douglas laughed. "Yeah, sorry. We have a lot more to tell you, I guess. The short version is that Gigi and I run an orphanage in Guatemala. It's our home and—well, we'll tell you all about it when we see you. And yes, of course I'll come there. I'm guessing it might be nice for your parents to meet me as well—before their daughter goes flying off to Italy to meet up with a bunch of strangers."

Isabelle heard a few muffled words on the other end of the line.

"Lia just walked in. She'd like to speak to you for a minute."

"Sure. I'd love to talk to her."

"Isabella? Gigi just filled me in with the good news. You're coming in a week?"

"It sounds like it. Thank you again for inviting me. I'm really looking forward to meeting you all."

"You have no idea how excited I am—how excited we all are to met you. So, I just walked in when I heard Douglas mentioning your parents, and I wanted to be sure to let you know that they should consider themselves invited as well. There's plenty of room for all of you here and we'd love to have you."

"Thank you so much. That's very kind of you."

Isabella would consider it, but her gut feeling was that she needed to do this trip on her own, knowing and assuming that there'd be plenty of time later for her parents to meet everyone.

"Okay, I'll let you go and I'll be counting the days until I get to meet my granddaughter. You have no idea how happy this has made me."

"Me too." Isabella's grin was wide.

"Gigi wants to talk to you for a minute. See you soon."

"Bye. See you soon."

"Isabella, honey, I'm so happy you're coming. You don't worry about a thing. Douglas is going to take good care of you and make sure you get to us safe and sound. You'll be here eating Lia's delicious homemade pasta before you know it. Bella, do you like Italian food?"

Isabella laughed at the question. "I love Italian. It's always been my favorite."

"Well, good, good. You're going to love it here. We'll see you soon, sweetie."

"Bye, Gigi.

Then Douglas was on the phone again to tell her that he'd arrange the flight, and e-mail her the details for it and his own travel plans so that they could arrange for their first meeting.

Isabella hung up the phone feeling a sense of excitement and an incredible peace. She didn't yet know much about her birth mother, but she did know one thing that was becoming more and more clear to her. Arianna had had an incredible group of people in her life who'd loved her very deeply until the day that she had died—and this same little family seemed to be opening their arms wide to Isabella now.

EIGHTEEN

Isabella smiled at Douglas sitting next to her as he reached over to hold her hand during take-off. She'd surprised herself so far in that she'd not felt the sense of panic that typically would send her racing to the restroom to throw up. She was nervous, but having Douglas there beside her was helping more than she'd even thought possible.

"Are you okay?"

She smiled in response. "I am nervous, but yeah. I'm gonna be okay."

She was more than okay. She was beyond excited to be taking her first trip out of the country—a trip that would bring her face-to-face with her grandparents on the other end of it.

The last few days had been a whirlwind of activity. Her parents had been supportive and seemed much more comfortable about Isabella leaving once they knew that they would be able to spend a little bit of time with Douglas.

She'd had a last meeting with Ms. Carlson, who'd been so proud of her for the decisions that she'd made since the last time they had spoken. Isabella still couldn't believe it herself. She'd already come such a long way from that over-anxious teenager who seemed to be working so hard to please everyone but herself. Now she was finally getting a sense of the things that made her happy, and it felt good to her to be making these decisions for herself.

She glanced over at Douglas. His eyes were closed and she wouldn't be surprised at all if he were asleep for most of the flight. As far as she could tell, he'd been on the go ever since they'd spoken on the phone about her coming. He'd been to Guatemala just for a few days before he got on a flight to Connecticut to meet with her. She smiled as she thought about how that first meeting had gone.

Isabella had gone to meet him in his hotel lobby, feeling nervous and excited to finally be meeting face-to-face with someone who had known her mother. From the moment they saw one another, every anxious thought had left her. His face had lit up when he saw her and she didn't miss his eyes filling with tears as he scooped her up into a big hug as if they'd known one another all her life. He'd wiped the tears from his eyes unapologetically, telling her that she looked just like her mother, and then they sat and talked for hours.

She reached down into her backpack to pull out the pictures Douglas had given her. The first was of Arianna and Lia. Douglas had told her that it was taken during a very special time that the two of them had spent together in Italy. Isabella smiled, thinking about how beautiful her mother was and that she did look like her. The resemblance was really amazing—even overwhelming—for Isabella, who had always felt the struggle of what it was like not to look like either of her parents.

There were pictures of Arianna with Blu and Jemma, the girl that Douglas had told her so much about who was studying to be an artist in Italy. Douglas thought that they would be fast friends. Isabella liked the way the young girl smiled in the picture, with just a hint of mischief—her blonde hair, blue eyes, and fair skin the exact physical opposite of Isabella's own dark hair, eyes, and skin tone.

And finally there was a picture of Lia with Antonio—her

grandparents, looking so happy standing in their vineyard on their wedding day. Douglas had explained a little bit about how they'd gotten together after so many years of being apart, but he'd said that Lia would probably want to share most of their love story herself with Isabella.

She knew that Blu also had a husband and a little girl name Kylie. And that Lia and Antonio had adopted Gabriela from the orphanage.

Isabella was starting to get a good feel for these people whom she was about to meet—these people who had known and loved her mother—and she couldn't be happier. It was the most unexpected gift that she ever could have imagined since the day that she'd been faced with the awful knowledge of Arianna's death. It didn't make up for the fact that she'd never have the chance to meet her birth mother, but it seemed to be giving her a sense of peace and closure that she never would have thought possible.

She felt her eyes filling with tears that she didn't bother to wipe away as she stared again at the picture of her mother and Lia. She knew those eyes. They were her own eyes looking back at her— without worry or regret. They were the eyes of a young girl who'd found happiness and contentment even amidst the hardships that had come her way so early in life.

Isabella looked over toward the window, suddenly realizing that somehow they were already flying high in the sky; she'd hardly even realized it once she'd gotten over her initial jitters.

She smiled as she thought about Thomas and how proud he was going to be of her for not throwing up once during the flight. They'd had a wonderful afternoon together the day before, ending in tears for both of them as it hit Isabella that most likely it would be a very long time until she'd see her best friend again—what with school for her, and Thomas being off on his own adventure for who knew how long.

In the back of her mind, Isabella had been entertaining the thought of meeting up with him in Europe later that summer after all. She no longer had the job or the money to worry about, and if she could handle the flight, there wouldn't be much keeping her from doing it. But she hadn't said anything to him yet because she wanted to be sure that the flight actually was manageable for her. Now she knew that it was, and surprisingly so.

Yes, she certainly had come a long way.

She felt Douglas stir beside her.

"How are you doing? Sorry, I must have dozed off there for a few seconds."

"I'm fine." She gave him a big smile. "Don't be sorry. You must be exhausted—all the traveling you've done these past few days. I'm just so thankful that you came out to fly with me. Really, Douglas, it means so much."

"I know it does, and I wouldn't have had it any other way. I am under strict orders by a couple of beautiful Italian women to deliver you safe and sound into their awaiting arms, and that's what I will do." He winked at her. "Be prepared for a serious Italian homecoming."

Isabella laughed. "I don't know exactly what that means but it sounds wonderful."

"Oh, it will be wonderful alright. Lots of tears and hugs, and then the food. Just be forewarned, I'm pretty sure Lia is cooking up a storm."

"Thanks for the warning."

Douglas had told her about Lia's restaurant, Thyme, and also about Chase, the other chef in the family. Isabella thought it sounded absolutely wonderful and couldn't wait to be in the kitchen with the two of them. She didn't know a lot about cooking, but it was always something that she wanted to learn more about, especially as it pertained to Italian food.

She was ready for Italy. She felt a shift, sure and steady within her.

Isabella was ready now for anything.

NINETEEN

Isabella laid her head back against the car seat in the sedan that had been awaiting their arrival in Florence. She watched the scenery out the window, fascinated at how different—how beautiful—it was. She turned to Douglas sitting beside her, smiling at her reaction.

"Wow. It's so pretty. Prettier than I imagined even."

"It never gets old—the views of Tuscany. Gigi and I come here at least once a year, and every time we marvel at the views. You know, you'll have to talk to Lia about when your mother came here for the first time. They made this same drive after spending several days in Florence together."

Isabella nodded, thinking about her mother, only a few years older than she was now, making this trip for the first and only time of her young life. The thought was both comforting and devastating to her.

"How are you feeling? You didn't sleep much during the flight. Are you tired?"

"I'm a little tired, but also excited. I'm sure I'll sleep well tonight, but for now I'm just feeling so excited to meet everyone."

Isabella was still feeling slightly shocked that the flight had gone as well for her as it had. She'd hardly experienced any anxiety at all, apart from just the initial jitters when they were taking off. Maybe her anxiety issues were finally behind her now. She smiled as she thought about the timing. It certainly felt like she was opening herself up to a more relaxed way of living. She was counting on this trip to Italy to help her even more with that.

Douglas looked at his phone as he received a text notification. "It's from Gigi. She's asking how much longer." He laughed. "Tonight you'll meet Lia, Antonio, their daughter Gabriela, and of course Gigi. Jemma's at a workshop in Rome and won't be in until very late tonight, so you probably won't meet her until the morning."

"And Blu? When did you say they were coming?"

"They'll be here early next week. I think they arrive on Tuesday and they'll stay for the remainder of your time here—we all will."

After some debate back and forth—mostly within Isabella's own mind about what would be a proper length for a visit—she'd decided to come to Italy for ten days. Lia had told her to come for as long as she liked—a month or the entire summer would be fine with them—but Isabella hadn't wanted to be gone that long from her parents. It felt like she'd be abandoning them, and even though they'd been so supportive and wonderful during the short time that they'd all spent with Douglas, Isabella knew that it had to be difficult for them to have her gone. She'd be away at college soon enough, so there was no need to do that to them any sooner than was necessary.

Isabella brought her attention back to Douglas, who was pointing ahead through the window.

"Here we are."

She sat mesmerized as they made their way up the long driveway toward the massive home she could see atop the hill. The whole scene looked like something out of a movie. It was just nearing that time of day when the sky turned into the most perfect shades of pastel colors, and outside the windows were miles of vineyard that stretched as far as she could see.

"Oh, it's so beautiful." She could hardly believe she was there.

"It is really gorgeous—one of the most beautiful properties I've seen in the area by far. Antonio had purchased the land prior to the time when he and Lia found one another again. They've done a lot of work on the villa and the whole property in the years since they've been married. Wait until you see the inside." He winked at her as the car pulled to a stop in front of the villa.

Before they could even take a step out of the car, Isabella saw them—Gigi was first, followed by Lia and Antonio who were hand-in-hand, all with big smiles and tears that Isabella didn't miss.

"You ready for this?" Douglas laughed, and Isabella didn't have a chance to respond before the driver was by her door, opening it wide for her to step out of the car and into the arms waiting to hug her.

Yes. She was ready.

She stepped out of the car and immediately the two women burst into tears, Antonio grinning widely behind them as they both rushed up to hug her.

"Bella, let me look at you."

"You must be Gigi." Isabella grinned at the woman who was just as Douglas had described her.

Gigi had her hands on either side of Isabella's face as she kissed one cheek and then the other. "I can't believe it. I can't believe how much you look like your mother. Doesn't she, Lia?"

Lia was standing off to the side, tears streaming down her face as she came to Isabella to do the same, giving her the biggest hug and speaking softly: "I have waited so long for this day. You are so beautiful, Isabella."

And then it was Antonio's turn. There was no mistaking the look on his face. Isabella knew that Antonio had had a hard time at first dealing with the fact that he'd not known that his daughter existed until after she was gone. Douglas had filled her in on that much of the story. And that he and Lia had moved past the hurt, he being left with pictures of Arianna and the memories that Lia had of those last months that she'd known her for such a brief time.

Now Antonio was hugging Isabella close, and she hadn't missed the tears in his eyes.

"Isabella, our beautiful girl. Let me look at you." He stepped back, creating a bit of space between them, Lia and Gigi still standing close, arm-in-arm.

"Come, come. Let's get you inside for some dinner," Lia finally interrupted. "Are you exhausted? Would you like to have a little rest first?"

"No. I think I'll be okay; maybe if I can just freshen up a bit?"

As she followed the women through the front door into the massive foyer, her breath caught. This villa she'd just stepped into was truly like something she'd only seen in the movies. Everything about it was gorgeous and magical.

"Oh my. Lia..." She felt a bit shy all of a sudden because she realized that she didn't know what to call Lia and Antonio, but by their first names seemed most appropriate. Lia was smiling next to her, linking her arm through hers.

"Yes?"

"Shall I call you Lia or..."

"Honey, you call me whatever you're comfortable with—and that goes for Antonio too, right, dear?"

Antonio nodded his head. "*Si*. I can be Antonio, Grandpa, or nonno."

"Italian for grandpa—and for grandma it's nonna. But you call us what you're comfortable with," said Lia.

Isabella nodded and followed the women into the kitchen while Antonio and Douglas left with her suitcases. "Something smells amazing in here. I've heard all about what to expect of your cooking, Lia."

"I'm so happy to cook for you." She smiled at Isabella and then took her hand to lead her through the kitchen into a massive hallway that seemed to go on forever. "Let me show you to your room. You can freshen up a bit and then we'll have a nice dinner together. Gabriela's over at a friend's house and they should be dropping her off in a few minutes. She's so excited to meet you too." She stopped and turned around to hug Isabella close. "Isabella, we're all so happy that you're here. It's like a small miracle after all these years and something none of us take lightly."

"I'm happy too. Really. The last few weeks have been so emotional for me and it feels good to be here now."

TWENTY

The room that Lia had put Isabella in was beautiful. She had her own balcony with views of the vineyard from each side of the property. She could barely make it out now because it was getting dark, but Lia assured her that the sunrise in the morning would be spectacular if she happened to be awake at an early hour.

Isabella made her way to the bathroom in the suite to splash some cold water on her face and brush her teeth. The smells of what seemed to be an Italian feast had made their way to her room and she was suddenly feeling ravenous. She changed into fresh clothes and made her way back downstairs.

Before she was all the way down the stairway, she saw a little girl running away into the dining room.

"She's coming, she's coming."

She could hear an excited little voice and it made her smile. Douglas had told her about Lia and Antonio falling in love with the then baby Gabriela when they'd first visited the orphanage. That had been over six years ago and Gabriela, now eight, had brought immense joy to their lives—to all of their lives.

The little girl popped back into the room just as Isabella reached the bottom of the staircase.

"Hi, Isabella." The child grinned and twirled around, making her colorful dress swish with the motion.

"Hi, Gabriela." Isabella smiled back.

"How do you know my name?"

"I've heard all about you. How do you know *my* name?" Isabella grinned.

"Mom and Dad said that you were coming. Oh, and know what?"

"What?"

"I'm actually your auntie." Gabriela burst into a fit of giggles, which made Isabella laugh as well.

"I guess that's true, isn't it?"

The child nodded and came over next to Isabella, reaching for her hand. "Are you ready to eat now? Mom is a very good cook, you know."

Isabella smiled at the very serious look on Gabriela's face. "So I've heard. And yes, I'm starving. Are you hungry?"

"Sure I am. Let's go."

Gabriela led Isabella into the dining room.

"Oh wow."

Isabella felt her stomach growl in response to the food she saw laid out before her. On the table were huge platters of meats, pastas, and salads. Everything looked incredible including Lia and Gigi in their aprons, rushing into the room with still more food.

"Sit, sit, bella," Gigi said as she motioned to Douglas, who immediately pulled out a chair in the center of the seating at the big table.

"Thank you. This all looks so delicious. I hope you all didn't go to too much trouble on account of me."

Douglas laughed. "Oh no. These women would cook up a storm any night of the week. If we didn't have a guest, we'd be inviting the neighbors or the tourists from the guest house down the road."

Antonio appeared carrying a bottle of wine and a pitcher of

water. "That's how we do it here in Tuscany." He leaned down to give Isabella a kiss on the cheek. "It's the Italian way."

Isabella laughed. "Well, I'm pretty sure I'm going to like it here in Italy."

"*Si*, I think it is who you are too, bella." He winked at her and Isabella felt the truth of the statement deep within her.

It was the confirmation that she was supposed to be here now, discovering more about who she was and about this little extended family that had meant so much to her birth mother. She felt completely at ease, comfortable around these new people in this house that was so completely foreign to her, yet seemed to also hold with it something known, maybe something she'd been searching for her entire life.

Finally Gigi and Lia seemed satisfied with the dishes that were on the table. Both women came over to kiss Isabella on the cheek once more before seating themselves—Lia across from her next to Antonio, who was already sitting down, and Gigi to her right.

Gabriela had already chosen her spot next to Isabella after moving the chair as close to her as was possible. Isabella grinned as she looked down at the child, who was now scooping some delicious-looking pasta onto Isabella's plate.

"Isabella, you have to try this. Mom makes the best Alfredo. I promise you are going to love it."

"Honey, I'm sure that Isabella might want to serve herself. Let's not completely overwhelm the poor girl."

Isabella and Antonio both laughed at the same time.

"No, it's fine. I love it. This food looks amazing, and I'm actually starving."

"Well, if you're looking to put on a few pounds for any reason, you've come to the right place. These women will feed you until you can't stuff another bite into your mouth." Douglas patted his stomach. "I'm proof of what happens every time Gigi and I come for a visit."

They all laughed and then, with a completely serious look on her face, Gabriela said, "It's the Italian way, Isabella."

This sent everyone into another round of laughter, and the welcome dinner was officially underway.

By the time they were only midway through dinner, Isabella felt as if she'd been coming there for years. Conversation and laughter flowed easily. She learned a great deal about the romance between her grandparents, and then Gigi and Lia told her stories about Arianna.

Between the conversations she'd already had with Douglas and listening to Gigi and Lia talk about their memories of Arianna, Isabella felt like she was finally starting to piece together what her mother's life had been like. It was especially emotional to talk about those last few months that Lia had had with her—to think about everything Arianna must have been feeling so close to the end of her life, but also to think about Lia as a mother herself, who'd finally reconnected with a daughter that she didn't know she was destined to lose long before they'd had enough time together.

She felt Gabriela's hand on her arm, startling her slightly as she realized that she'd been lost in her thoughts for several seconds.

"Are you okay, Isabella?"

Isabella thought how sweet the little girl was as she quickly wiped the tears away with the sleeve of her shirt. She hadn't even realized how emotional she'd become—how much hearing the stories of her mother had affected her.

"Yeah, I'm okay, sweetie. I think I'm just tired. It's been a very long day."

Douglas was nodding. "Don't let us keep you, Isabella. There'll be plenty of time for more stories and long chats."

"Thank you." Isabella looked around the table at the new faces who, after only a few hours, didn't seem like strangers to her any more. Was it really possible that she could feel so comfortable so fast? So much about this experience that she seemed to be having was foreign to her—not just the physical location, but the feelings she was having and the ease with which she almost instantly felt a sense of belonging.

As quickly as she had the thought, she remembered that she'd promised to send her parents a text once she'd arrived. They'd be anxious to know that the flight had gone well and that Isabella was safe and sound at her destination. She stifled a yawn.

"Yes, I suppose I am feeling quite sleepy all of a sudden. But I can't wait to talk more and hear all about the vineyard and the orphanage as well. It's all so different and exciting to me."

Lia and Gigi stood up from their chairs to come around to her side of the table as she stood. She hugged them both as if it was the most natural thing in the world to do, and Lia walked her upstairs to her room.

Before Lia turned to go, she grabbed Isabella for one more hug, speaking quietly in her ear. "I'm so happy to have you here, bella. It really is my dream come true. Nothing in the world could have made me happier. I just want you to know that."

Isabella saw her grandmother's eyes filled with tears as she felt her own well up also. This was her grandmother—her flesh and blood—and it was something that was also a dream come true for her.

"Me too." Isabella kissed her on the cheek and they said goodnight.

TWENTY-ONE

Isabella stepped out onto the balcony of her room, stretching high and breathing in the cool morning air. For as far as she could see, it looked like vineyard after vineyard, and it was simply breathtaking. She'd thought momentarily about going for a run—she'd brought her running shoes—but then she saw someone who could only be Jemma out on the terrace below. She looked deeply engrossed in whatever she was painting at her easel.

Isabella watched her intently for several minutes. She was the little blonde girl from the pictures all grown up, her shoulder-length blonde hair blowing in the light breeze, her hands making sweeping strokes across the paper with colors that seemed to perfectly match what Isabella was seeing in the morning sky before her eyes.

Douglas had told Isabella about Jemma during their flight, mentioning that she'd recently gone through a rough time—which was why she'd come to be staying with Lia and Antonio at the vineyard. Isabella thought the way that Douglas talked about Jemma was incredibly sweet, as if she were his own family. It wasn't hard to imagine, given the time that Jemma had spent with Gigi and Douglas, that she must feel the same way about them.

Isabella was anxious to meet her and it seemed like now might be just that opportunity.

She grabbed her hoodie and sneakers from her suitcase and quietly slipped down the stairs to the outside patio.

As Isabella slid the sliding door open to go outside, Jemma looked up from her painting, setting her paintbrush down and taking the few short steps to meet her across the patio.

"Hi, you must be Isabella." She walked closer and surprised Isabella by grabbing her in a hug. "It's so great to meet you finally. I'm Jemma."

Isabella loved her smile and the energy that seemed to radiate from her.

"Hi, it's great to meet you too. I've heard a lot of nice things about you."

"Oh, yeah?"

Isabella laughed. "Is that surprising?"

"No, not really. Well, especially not if it's coming from Gigi and Douglas. Seriously though, I did tell Douglas to feel free to fill you in on everything that's happened with me recently, so I'm sure you already know what they've done for me. I'm pretty much an open book these days anyway—but I wanna hear everything about you. Do you want a coffee?"

She was already heading into the kitchen, so Isabella followed her back inside.

Jemma made them two wonderfully strong-smelling Italian coffees and they carried them back out to the patio.

"It's so beautiful here," Isabella said, as she took in the full scope of the view revealed to her now in the light of day.

"I know. I love it here so much. I've been coming here since I was a little girl and I never get tired of it. It's still feeling a bit surreal to me that I'm actually living here right now."

"I'll bet. I mean, I can only imagine what that would feel like."

"Well, you know, I mostly feel incredibly lucky to have people like Lia and Antonio and Gigi and Douglas in my life. They're good people, Isabella. You're gonna find that out too." Jemma was smiling and seemed so sure of herself.

"I feel lucky too. I mean, it was so devastating when I first found out that my birth mother—that Arianna had died—I never dreamed that I'd get more than the logistics about her life, but meeting you all—it's just been more than I could have ever imagined. The stories that Lia and Gigi were telling me last night—I'm just really thankful that I have at least that, you know?"

Isabella shocked herself a bit with the tears that were flowing in front of this girl who was virtually a stranger to her, but Jemma was quick to reach her hand out to grab Isabella's.

"Hey, I can only imagine." She looked down for a moment as she sipped her coffee. "I was only six when Ari died—I guess the same age as you were. I do have some wonderful memories. She really loved me a lot. I remember that about her."

Isabella's tears stopped. "I'd love to hear anything that you have to tell me."

Jemma went on to tell her about jelly beans, nicknames, convertible rides with the top down, and the loud opera music that Arianna had loved. Gigi and Lia had said similar things the night before. In just the short time that Isabella had already been here, she was starting to get a picture of who her mother was before she died.

"So tell me about you." Jemma asked, looking at Isabella intently. "Douglas says that you're starting school at Harvard in the fall, so I guess that means you're pretty smart, huh?"

Isabella felt her face grow warm. She wasn't always comfortable talking about herself and certainly didn't want to come off as if she were bragging about anything.

"I am going to Harvard, yeah. I'm going on a scholarship, but I don't know that I'm overly smart or anything. I have to work pretty hard at it—keeping my grades up, I mean."

Jemma was watching her as she sipped her coffee. "I don't think you're bragging—if you're worried about that. I mean, you can be totally straight with me. I probably could have gone to a good school too—I certainly had the money to be able to afford it —well, you do too with your trust. But I dunno. I didn't really think college was for me—not yet anyway."

When Isabella had found out that Arianna had also left Jemma a trust fund, it had intrigued her. Her birth mom had obviously felt quite a connection to the young girl and her mother whom Isabella had yet to meet. Now, as she studied her, she felt more of a connection with her than she could even explain. It wasn't normal for her to open up quickly to people, but she felt oddly comfortable with Jemma.

"Did you feel any pressure? To go to school?" Isabella asked. She got the sense that Jemma was very free-spirited and would never let things cause her stress the way that Isabella did.

"No, not really. Honestly, though, I think my mom and Chase were just happy that I didn't end up on the street somewhere—or worse, dead." She shrugged, but Isabella had the feeling that there was a lot of truth to her statement.

Isabella wondered just how bad things had gotten for Jemma. Douglas hadn't really gone into detail, but he did mention that she'd had a close call that had landed her in the emergency room right before she'd gone to stay with them at the orphanage.

"So are you having any regrets? About not going to school?" Isabella asked; for some reason Jemma's answer to the question was very important to her.

Jemma grinned. "Not in the least. I love it here. And I'm learning so much about art. It's been really good for me. My mom says that I was born to be an artist, so in that respect I guess I'm pretty lucky. She's super creative too, so she's always been really supportive of that. What about your parents? What do they think about all this—about you coming here?"

"For the most part, they've been really supportive and they are —in general, I suppose." Isabella took a sip of her coffee and wondered how much she should open up. "I did feel a lot of pressure growing up—to get good grades, get into a good school, and even to become a lawyer but..." Her voice trailed off and she noticed Jemma looking at her intently.

"But what? You can tell me anything. Really. I won't judge you."

"Well, I'm just starting to wonder if maybe some of this pressure that I've been feeling for so long has been in my own head. Maybe my parents would be proud of me no matter what I did."

"I bet that's true." Jemma said this as though it were a fact. "Is there something else you want to do?" Isabella must have had a confused look on her face. "Other than become a lawyer, I mean? That's what you're talking about, isn't it?"

Isabella felt stunned for a moment. "I don't know."

"Well, if you did know what would your answer be?" Jemma laughed.

"I do like to write." Isabella answered the question quietly.

"Well then?"

"Actually I love to write—more than anything else." Isabella grinned.

"So, are you a lawyer or a writer?" Jemma smiled. "Maybe that's something you should try to figure out while you're here."

Isabella nodded, feeling something inside her shift ever so slightly. Was she a lawyer or a writer? Could it really be that simple?

They sat in silence for several minutes, finishing their coffees before Jemma got up from the table. "Wanna come see my painting?"

Isabella nodded and followed her over to the easel. She couldn't believe how much she'd already opened up to Jemma. It felt as if they'd been friends for years. She wasn't used to having girlfriends, and something about it felt intensely gratifying.

TWENTY-TWO

Castellina in Chianti was everything that Isabella had pictured whenever she'd thought about Italy. She'd gotten up early to go to the market with Lia before she'd finally been introduced to the restaurant—to Thyme. Lia had told Isabella about the day that she and Arianna had come upon it and about the many meals that they'd shared together there. They'd even retraced the steps that Arianna and Lia had taken in the small village the day that they'd first discovered the restaurant.

Isabella met Carlo, who was now retired, and Sofia, who was the manager of the restaurant. They'd arrived just after the lunch rush, and Lia had slipped back into the kitchen to make them one of her favorite pasta dishes.

Isabella walked over to one wall of the restaurant that was covered with photos. It seemed to be a wall of memories of all the parties and good times that had taken place at Thyme throughout the years. Many of the photos included Gigi and Douglas, and Jemma with her family.

Isabella studied a picture of Blu and Jemma. Blu was the last piece of this little family puzzle to meet, and Isabella was looking forward to it. She imagined that Arianna's best friend might have some different insights for her about her birth mother.

In the center of the wall was a large picture of Arianna. Isabella studied it. The picture had been taken outside somewhere. Arianna's hair was blowing in the wind, her smile wide and her eyes bright. Isabella thought that she looked very happy.

"She was really beautiful wasn't she?"

Isabella turned to Lia, who'd come up behind her.

"She was." Isabella was thoughtful for a few seconds. "Do you really think I look like her?" She felt her face grow warm. "I mean, I'm not asking because we're talking about how beautiful she is or anything."

Lia put her arm around her granddaughter's waist. "I think you look almost exactly like her. And you are very beautiful, bella. Hasn't anyone ever told you that?"

Isabella had to think about the question for a few seconds. She'd not grown up thinking that she was particularly beautiful or not beautiful. It had just always been a non-issue for her.

She flashed to a memory of her and her mom being approached by a man at the mall when she was about twelve. He'd looked at Isabella very intently as he gave her mom a business card and later, when she'd asked her mom what the man had wanted, she'd only said that it wasn't something for young girls—that it was too much pressure for a young girl. She knew now that the man had been a scout for a modeling agency, and she had to laugh because she'd had a whole other world of pressure created around her—one that she felt couldn't have been any less stressful than that of being a child model.

She turned to Lia now to respond. "I don't know about being beautiful but I do like it that I look like her. It's kind of amazing to me, really."

Lia leaned in to kiss her on the cheek. "I like that too."

Isabella smiled in return and followed Lia to the small table where she'd set their pasta down.

"Has anyone told you that Arianna bought Thyme for me?"

"Time?" Isabella didn't understand what Lia was telling her.

"The restaurant. It was part of the inheritance that Arianna left me."

Isabella shook her head. They'd talked about the restaurant a lot but hadn't gotten around to talking about how Lia had come to own it.

"I can remember being here with her almost as if it were yesterday. Even though we hadn't spent that much time together—not in the sense of actual days—we learned so much about one another during that time, especially when we were here in Italy together."

Isabella was nodding, taking it all in. "So my mother knew that you'd want the restaurant?"

Lia smiled. "Ari knew that it had been a dream of mine when I was younger—to own a restaurant. It was a dream that I'd given up on long before we'd reunited. She was very thoughtful in planning everything that she'd prepared for each of us—you included, Isabella. I want you to know that.

"Like Jemma's, your trust fund was set up to help you realize your dreams—whatever that looks like for you. Ari was very clear with me about letting you know this. So for you—I'd imagine this will really help you with college. I know you have a scholarship, but I'd think there would be plenty of other expenses and you won't have to work. You can focus on your studies."

Isabella was thoughtful.

"What is it?"

"I can't even tell you what that amount of money will mean for me at school. Nothing about coming here—about contacting Douglas—has been about the money, but I can see now after meeting you all and hearing about my mother's wishes, that what she'd set up for me meant a lot to her. For that reason, it's starting to mean more to me too. I mean, just that it's got me thinking more about my dreams and about the things that I may have wanted for my life if money wasn't an obstacle."

"I wanna hear more about these dreams of yours." Lia winked at her and Isabella would have had a hard time putting what she was feeling to words in that moment.

Isabella opened up to her grandmother as they ate their lunch, sharing things with her that she'd only ever shared with Thomas and Ms. Carlson. She told her about some of the pressure she'd been feeling and also about her love of writing. She even shared her dreams of travel and how, now that she felt confident that she could handle flying, she felt that maybe this trip to Italy just might be the first of many trips for her. Now that she wouldn't have to worry about working during the summer months, she could easily see herself spending future summers there in Italy with her grand-parents.

"Sorry, I know I'm talking a lot." Isabella laughed, thinking it was the understatement of the year. She felt like she'd never talked this much to people she'd only just met—ever. It was strange and felt oddly right.

Lia reached across the table to grab her hand. "Don't you apol-ogize to me for anything of the sort. You have no idea how much our conversations mean to me. To be honest, I'm going to have a very hard time seeing you go." She squeezed Isabella's hand. "I want it to be very clear that you are more than welcome to stay here with us for as long as you like. If you wanted to move in, we've got a wing of the villa just waiting for you."

They both laughed and Isabella's heart felt full. She did know how welcome she was here, but she also felt a twinge of guilt because as much as she might like to stay, she'd never do it without considering her parents back home. They'd been texting and she'd already spoken to them twice on the phone, even doing a video chat to show them around the villa and introduce them to everyone.

"Thank you, Lia—Grandma." Isabella felt a bit shy, but it felt right to call Lia Grandma. "And I do feel welcome here. I guess I'll just take it one step at a time right now, enjoying this next week that I still have with you all. I'm excited to meet Blu and the rest of Jemma's family."

Her grandmother's smile widened. "Yes, it will be a real celebration when they arrive. I know how excited Blu is to meet you and I know that Jemma already thinks a great deal of you. Having you young women around here is good for Grandpa and me."

Isabella laughed and dug into her pasta for a last big bite. "Well, as if your warm welcome and hospitality weren't enough, I must say that your cooking is going to have me spoiled rotten for good Italian food forever."

"Now you let me know anytime you want to join me in the kitchen for some lessons. I love to cook and I love to teach—as does Chase, whom you'll meet very soon, by the way. Nothing would please us more than to have a couple of sous chefs to pass some of our favorite recipes down to. My guess is that you have the Italian cooking gene, anyway." Lia winked at her.

"Did Ari—did my mother like to cook?"

"You know, she didn't really cook growing up." Lia looked thoughtful. "And she and I only had a very few occasions to cook together, but I think she loved being in the kitchen with me. I know that I loved having her there."

Isabella loved the way her grandmother looked whenever she told Isabella stories about her times with Arianna. She made a mental note to be sure to allocate that time in the kitchen with her before she left. She smiled as she thought about it. Isabella wanted to know herself if she had that Italian cooking gene—if it was possible that she'd inherited any of that natural skill that her grandmother seemed to possess.

TWENTY-THREE

Isabella curled up on the small sofa in her room and waited for Thomas to pick up his phone. They'd been playing phone tag and she'd not spoken to him since before she'd left. She was anxious to fill him in and tell him about everyone that she'd met so far in Italy.

"Izzy! My long-lost best friend!"

Isabella laughed, delighted to hear her friend's voice. "I know. It's good to finally talk to you too. How are you?"

"Oh, you know. All the same here, but how are you? How was the flight? How's Italy? How was it meeting your grandparents? Tell me everything."

Isabella laughed at all the questions he was firing at her. "The flight—can you believe I hardly even paid attention to the fact that we were in the air? I was a little anxious right before take-off, but having Douglas there was great. And of course we had tons to talk about. so I didn't have a lot of time to think about the fact that I was finally on an airplane."

Isabella knew that Thomas understood what a big fear this was to have conquered. She hadn't thought a lot about it because she'd had so much else on her mind, but she could now easily imagine herself flying again. This was a very big deal, and talking about it now with Thomas was like a light bulb going off in her head. What did this really mean for her life?

"I knew you could do it—well, I knew you would do it anyway, but that's great, Iz. Really. And how's Italy? Do you love it?"

"Thomas, it's so gorgeous here. You can't believe where Lia and Antonio—where my grandparents live. It's the most fantastic huge villa on top of a hill and it looks over their entire vineyard. It looks pretty much like what you'd imagine Italy to look like. I'll have to bring you sometime. I'm sure that they would love that. Honestly, they've made me feel so welcome it's unbelievable, really. I feel as though I've been coming here my whole life."

She could hear Thomas laughing on the other end of the line. "So, I take it you're enjoying meeting them all then. No weirdness, huh?"

"Nope, not at all. I've met my grandparents—oh, and they've got a daughter—Gabriela, who's eight. You know how I told you that Gigi and Douglas run an orphanage in Guatemala? They adopted her from there when she was a baby." Isabella stopped to catch her breath, realizing that she was talking nonstop.

"What about the girl that's our age? What was her name?"

"Oh, yeah. Jemma. She's really great—and such a good artist. I feel like we're gonna be pretty good friends. I just met her a few days ago and we've been hanging out a bit every day since then. Her mom and the rest of her family are coming in tomorrow. I think I told you that her mom—Blu—well, actually she's really Jemma's sister but she raised her—anyway, Blu was my mom's best friend."

Thomas was laughing again. "This sounds like a very interesting group of people. I'm really glad that you're enjoying your time with them, Iz. You know, I'm not being overly dramatic when I say that I've not seen you this excited since—well, I was going to say ever, but maybe since the day you first got the idea of going to Harvard into your head."

Isabella's heart beat faster at the mention of Harvard and she didn't know exactly why. She brushed the feeling aside.

"Well, it is all very exciting, I guess. It's more than I ever imagined anyway. That's for sure. I mean, I fully intended to find out everything I could about my birth mother and that is happening for sure, but I..." Isabella had to stop for a moment to clear her throat, overcome by sudden emotion. "I just never would have imagined that I'd see myself feeling so comfortable with them this fast. They really do feel like family to me. Sorry to get so emotional on you."

"Nah, you know you don't have to apologize to me about that —not ever. I'm happy for you. And I miss you. I'm really kinda counting on seeing you late this summer now, so I hope this trip is going to give you the travel bug."

Isabella laughed. "There's a good chance of that, I'd say."

Isabella heard a light knock on her door. "Come in."

Jemma stuck her head in the door. "Lia's got a snack for us outside when you're ready."

"One sec, Thomas." Isabella put her hand over the phone.

"Oh, sorry. I didn't realize you were on the phone," said Jemma.

"No problem. Be down in five minutes?"

Jemma nodded and shut the door.

Isabella turned her attention back to Thomas on the phone. "Sorry about that. Lia's been cooking the most delicious food. I swear I'm gonna come back ten pounds heavier."

"You'd look fine if you put on a little weight, Iz—not that you don't look great now. But I'm jealous of the food. That sounds so great." Thomas laughed. "I wanna be in Italy with you."

"You'll be in Europe soon enough. And I miss you. I'm glad we finally connected."

"Me too. Keep me posted."

"Will do. Bye."

Isabella clicked off her phone and changed into a pair of jeans. She put her hair up in a ponytail and made her way downstairs.

TWENTY-FOUR

Isabella sat upstairs in her room writing in her journal. Journaling was something she missed when she wasn't doing it every day, and she'd been so busy since she'd arrived in Italy that she'd skipped a few days. Now she was finally getting caught up with her thoughts about being there and first impressions of everyone that she'd met.

Today was the day that she was going to finally meet Blu, who was due to arrive any minute. Isabella was slightly nervous but mostly excited. She'd talked to her on the phone the day before when Jemma had called Blu, and from what everyone had been telling her, Blu was very anxious to meet her too.

She turned her thoughts back to her writing. She'd been feeling very creative ever since she'd arrived in Tuscany—maybe it was the beautiful scenery, maybe it was watching Jemma painting outside. She'd been having some character ideas for a few stories that were in her head. She'd canceled her writing class before she'd left home for Italy but she could pick up another one when she got back. In the meantime, she'd been working on a few ideas, thankful that she'd packed her laptop at the last minute.

She saw a red convertible pulling up the driveway and knew that it was Blu. Jemma had told her that when they had the time, her mom and Chase loved to rent a car and make the drive from Florence to the villa. Isabella watched out the window as Gabriela ran outside to the car and soon after she watched as a little girl who could only be Jemma's sister, Kylie, got out, followed by Blu and Chase. Isabella felt her heart pounding. Blu was the last of the missing pieces in the puzzle that was her connection to her mother.

She heard the footsteps running up the stairs and then down the hallway, stopping outside her door, followed by loud giggles that made her smile.

There was a quiet tap at her door.

"Who is it?" She smiled in anticipation of meeting Jemma's little sister, Gabriela's good friend that she'd been talking about to Isabella for days.

"It's me. Gabriela."

She heard whispers.

"And me...I'm Kylie."

"Isabella, can we come in please?" Gabriela said.

"Yes, please."

Isabella set her journal down and got up in anticipation of meeting the two little girls across the room as they burst in, all smiles and still giggling.

"Isabella, this is my friend Kylie."

The little blonde girl stuck her hand out toward Isabella. "I'm very pleased to meet you, Isabella. I've heard a lot of very nice things about you." She grinned and Isabella thought how adorable she looked with two of her front teeth missing.

Isabella shook her hand. "Likewise. I'm pleased to meet you too, and I've also heard a lot of nice things about you. You girls sure are very polite, aren't you?"

Kylie giggled. "Isabella, please tell that to our mothers."

Isabella laughed. These two kids were cracking her up.

"Do you want to go down to meet Kylie's parents now?" asked Gabriela.

"Sure."

She followed the two girls down the stairway and into the kitchen, where everyone seemed to be congregating.

Blu turned around just as they entered, and her hand covered her mouth. "Oh wow." She burst into tears and took the few steps forward to pull Isabella in for a big hug.

Isabella, a bit stunned, hugged her back, thinking how this emotional reaction didn't fit the idea of who she thought Blu would be. She'd spent a little time online, watching some interviews that Blu had done at various fashion events and she always seemed very put together and quite edgy, unlike the woman who now held her in her arms as she cried.

Blu took a step back now, holding Isabella at arm's length, looking at her intently as she seemed to be sizing her up from head to toe. But it didn't really make Isabella uncomfortable because she appreciated the honesty of the moment.

Finally Blu's tears stopped and she stood holding Isabella's hand. Isabella could see that Jemma had entered the kitchen and stood quietly to the side watching the scene with a smile on her face, as was the case with everyone else nearby.

"I'm so sorry, Isabella." Blu finally spoke. "I had no idea that seeing you was going to affect me like this. You just—you look so much like Arianna. It's absolutely incredible. It's as if I'm being transported back in time and it's your mother standing in front of me."

Isabella smiled at Blu, feeling oddly relaxed despite the emotional scene that had just taken place. "There's no need to apologize. I've been feeling pretty emotional about meeting you also." She leaned in to give her a hug. "And it's really great to meet you. I'm guessing that my mother would have been pleased that this day has come."

"Arianna would be beside herself," Gigi said, tears streaming down her face. "She wanted this so much—for us all to meet you. And we've wanted it too."

"I say it's cause for an Italian celebration," Kylie said from the corner of the room, where she was holding onto Jemma's hand.

The grown-ups laughed and as if on cue, Lia and Gigi started grabbing platters of food that were already laid out on the counter.

Jemma kissed Kylie on the forehead. "That, my dear sister, is a fantastic idea. Why don't you and Gabriela get the napkins and I'll start setting the table outside."

Isabella was introduced to Chase, and the two of them along with Blu made their way out to the patio. She liked the couple right away as they settled into easy conversation, assured by the others that the lunch preparations were taken care of—that they should spend a little time getting to know one another.

By the time lunch was served, Isabella had heard several stories about Arianna, including how she'd been responsible for Blu and Chase meeting all those years ago. Blu had laughed about it, saying that especially for that last year of Ari's life, she'd been very busy playing matchmaker for both her and Gigi—two matches that Isabella and anyone could see had been perfect.

It was becoming clearer and clearer to Isabella that Arianna had had a huge impact on the lives of these people who loved her —an impact that was felt long after her death and one that also didn't have to do only with the physical things that she'd left for those she loved.

TWENTY-FIVE

Isabella looked over at Blu where she sat in the driver's seat of the convertible. It was a perfect day for a ride with the top down—that was what Blu had said earlier that morning when she knocked quietly on Isabella's door to see if she was up for a drive to the coast. Isabella didn't have to think twice about her answer. She was anxious to get to know this woman who had been such a big part of her mother's life; plus a drive through Tuscany sounded fantastic.

They drove in silence but it didn't feel awkward to Isabella at all. Blu glanced over at her, smiling widely.

"Honestly, I can't get over it, Isabella. I hope I'm not making you feel strange. It's just that you look so much like her. I can't tell you the number of times I rode with your mom, driving her red convertible over the Golden Gate Bridge for a drive just like the one we're taking. For some reason, she always loved riding in the passenger seat and I always did love driving her car, so it worked for both of us." She laughed and Isabella smiled in response.

She liked thinking about her mother riding in a car like this one, the sun on her face and the wind whipping her hair around just as it was doing with Isabella's now.

"What else did my mom like?"

Blu looked thoughtful. "I'll show you one of her greatest loves. Jemma thinks it's kind of weird when I do this because she knows it's not my music at all, but it reminds me of Arianna and I like to remember her—especially when I'm in San Francisco but also here in Italy."

They pulled over to the side of the road so that Blu could connect her phone to the car speaker system. She pulled up the music she was looking for as Isabella waited, curious as to what it was going to be.

"We used to argue about our music selection and then we'd compromise by each getting a say for one way of a trip, but Ari always wanted hers loud and she always loved the top down."

Isabella saw Blu brush a tear away quickly before she pressed play and turned it up loud as they pulled away to continue their drive. Isabella rested her head back against the seat, letting the opera music overwhelm her senses.

Maybe it was the fact that they were driving in Italy, or maybe it was a combination of everything else she'd learned about her mother this past week, but Isabella didn't have a hard time imagining Arianna loving this music that she herself found so beautiful now, even though she'd barely listened to opera before.

Several tracks played before Blu reached over to turn the music down.

"So what do you think about everything, Isabella? I imagine it might be more than a little overwhelming for you—that we might all be a little overwhelming for you." She laughed.

Isabella thought about the question for several seconds before she replied. She'd gone through so many different emotions the past few weeks, and she was learning to be more honest about her feelings—with others, but maybe even more importantly with herself.

"At first, you know, I was so angry with my parents—about the fact that they'd kept the truth from me about Arianna's death. It was pretty devastating to find out the way that I did."

Blu looked quickly over at Isabella. "Jemma told me that she's filled you in on our story—about the things that I'd kept from her."

"Oh no, I wasn't saying—" Isabella felt her face getting warm. The last thing she wanted was for Blu to feel judged by her.

"Oh, no worries about that. I know you're not talking about us. I'm just bringing it up because I guess maybe I can sympathize with your parents—about the decisions that they've made regarding the timing of giving you information about Arianna. Believe me, it pained us all to have to wait to see if and when the day would come when we'd finally get a chance to get to know you."

"Oh, I know what you're saying. And I've forgiven my parents. Really. I mean, it was hard at first, but I do understand. It was more just the shock of it all, ya know—because I guess—I always thought that one day I'd meet her—I'd meet my birth mother. It's pretty much always been in the back of my mind, so that's the part that was difficult. I finally had to let go of that hope that I always had."

"I can only imagine." Blu reached over to grab hold of Isabella's hand, giving it a squeeze. "Arianna talked about you a lot, Isabella. She never forgot about the day that you were born, and I know that she thought about you every day since then. She did live with a lot of regret about that day, and I know that she wanted you to know that it wasn't her choice to give you up. She had forgiven her adoptive parents too, but nonetheless, their relationship had never been good after that time in her life. There was too much hurt and anger there. And she did feel a lot of guilt for not being stronger, not trying to enforce her own wish to keep you herself."

Isabella felt a lump in her throat and had to take a few moments before she could ask the question that was on her mind. "Do you think that she'd forgiven them at the time of her passing?

Do you think that she'd been able to forgive herself? Or was it something that she'd hung on to?"

Blu seemed thoughtful. "No, she'd forgiven them. Gigi would be the one to talk to about that. Shortly before she passed, they'd spent some time together talking about her parents, and I think Ari had come to a real point of understanding with it all and maybe, more importantly, a point of forgiveness—for her sake, I mean."

"That's good to know. I've spent a lot of time thinking about what it must have been like for her—to be faced with such hardship so young. Any hurt or anger I've had toward my parents can't compare to what she must have gone through losing her parents and then being faced with her own death. It's hard to imagine how anyone my age could have handled that. I mean, she was only a few years older than I am now."

Blu was nodding her head. "Well, I can tell you that Ari changed a lot during those last months of her life—since the death of her parents, really. She was my best friend so I loved her and everything, but some people would have certainly called her spoiled, for lack of a better description." Blu laughed, but it was something that Gigi had alluded to earlier also. "I knew a different side of her, though—I mean, I never would have been friends with someone like that if she hadn't shown me her true heart. And Ari did have a huge heart. She was one of the most loyal people I've ever known."

They were both quiet for a few seconds. Isabella loved hearing everything about Arianna, and it was refreshing to hear even the things that weren't so flattering. It made her seem more real. They'd all done a very good job of being honest with her about her mother just as Blu was being honest with her now, and she was extremely grateful for that.

"Anyway, as I was saying, Arianna learned a lot during those last months of her life and it changed her. I think meeting Lia—meeting your grandmother—was what brought her to a place of forgiveness and a place of being able to go feeling like her life had been worthwhile. Even though some people would have called her spoiled when she was younger, Arianna was incredibly generous. No one who really knew her would have suggested otherwise. But I guess toward the end especially, she just seemed to put her entire focus on others—on all of us for sure, but also she realized that the greatest peace she could feel was what came from forgiving herself, and she was able to do that. I really believe it. So you shouldn't think twice about any of that—if it's been on your mind, okay?"

Isabella nodded, feeling thoughtful about everything that had just been said. It was more pieces to the puzzle fitting into place. Every day she was getting a more complete picture of who her mother had been, and she liked the woman that she was getting to know through these people who had loved her mother so much.

Isabella's thoughts returned to Blu's question about feeling overwhelmed there in Italy.

"Being here with you all doesn't feel overwhelming to me as much as it feels like a huge gift. From the moment I first spoke to Douglas and the others on the phone, I felt sure that I wanted to meet you all. Something about it just felt so right and now that I'm here, it feels natural—almost as if I've been hanging out here with you all for years. I love that—probably more than I can express." She felt tears stinging her eyes. It was hard to explain in words what these past days had meant to her. It had gone better than she ever could have imagined and for the last few days, especially, she was almost having a hard time contemplating leaving.

Blu smiled widely. "Well, I know that I speak on behalf of everyone when I say that your presence here and in each of our lives is something we've wanted for a very long time. You've made your grandparents so very happy. Honestly, I've not seen Lia this happy since her wedding."

Isabella grinned too. She believed what Blu was telling her.

"And I really like Jemma. I've never had a lot of girlfriends, so it feels good to connect with her."

"She likes you too. And Jemma hasn't had a lot of good girl-friends either—not for the past few years anyway. I think you two might be really good for one another." Blu seemed to get slightly choked up.

"My mother would have liked that, wouldn't she? That Jemma and I are becoming friends?"

"Arianna would have loved that. She and Jemma had a very special relationship, but you know, at first she almost couldn't be around her—because it reminded her of you and what she'd lost."

"But Jemma won her over, I guess, and I'm glad she did." Isabella smiled.

"I'm glad too." Blu looked thoughtful for a few seconds. "Now shall we listen to the rest of *La Boheme?*—this was Ari's favorite, by the way." Blu smiled and reached for the volume knob.

Isabella laid her head back against the seat, listening to what had been her mom's favorite opera as they continued the drive without speaking.

TWENTY-SIX

Isabella waited outside on the patio for Gigi to bring the coffee and scones that she'd been smelling since she'd woken up that morning. She'd gotten into the habit of waking up early enough to catch a beautiful sunrise in the morning, and normally Jemma would be up and painting at this time too. Yesterday Jemma had gone to a workshop in Florence, so this morning it was only Isabella and Gigi awake so early.

Everyone had raved about her scones, and Gigi herself had joked about it being the one Italian dish that she'd mastered, although both Douglas and Lia were quick to correct her. Isabella learned that Gigi had been quite a good student in the years since she and Douglas had married when it came to expanding her cooking abilities.

Isabella looked down at the text she'd just gotten from her father, telling her that they couldn't wait to see her in a few days. She quickly texted him back as Gigi set the tray of scones and coffee down on the table in front of her.

"Gigi, those smell delicious."

"These were your mother's favorites since she was a little girl.

Well, unless she was just trying to humor me, of course, which is entirely possible." Gigi laughed.

"I doubt it. Your scones seem to have a reputation." Isabella smiled as she picked up the still warm scone from the plate in front of her and nibbled the end off it. "Delicious."

Gigi was looking at her intently, smiling, and Isabella knew without asking that it was because she was thinking about Arianna as she watched her eat. She hadn't yet really had a moment to talk to Gigi alone, and she was hoping that she could ask her some questions about Arianna's childhood.

"Gigi?"

"Yes, my darling girl."

"Will you tell me about my mother? What she was like when she was young? Was she a happy child?"

Gigi picked up a scone and settled back into her chair.

"I think she was, yes. She certainly didn't want for anything. There were parties and summer camps and many trips to the beach house in the summer. She was a pretty busy young girl."

"Okay..." Isabella was thinking that busy didn't necessarily equate to happy, but she didn't want to put words in Gigi's mouth. She'd heard from Blu already that Arianna didn't exactly have parents that were overly involved in her life. She already knew that many of Arianna's best times when she'd been little had had to do with Gigi's being there with her for it all.

"I guess that you played such a big role in her upbringing that if she was happy, much of that would be attributed to you."

Gigi seemed a bit embarrassed, and Isabella had the over-whelming urge to put her mind at ease.

"I'm so glad that my mother had you in her life. I've grown up around very wealthy families from my high school and I know what that environment can be like—not that all wealthy families are like that, but I've seen enough to know that often it's the nannies, the tutors, and the housekeepers that play the biggest roles in the lives of the kids. And I'm just really thankful that you were there for Arianna."

Isabella saw the tears that came fast to Gigi's eyes as she reached across the table for Isabella's hand. "Bella, you are really a sweet soul, you know that?"

It was Isabella's turn to blush. "I love it when you call me Bella."

Gigi looked at her for several seconds before she spoke. "I can't believe that your name is Isabella. When I heard what your name was—when Douglas read it to us from the e-mail you sent just a few short weeks ago—I thought my heart was going to burst with the sweet irony of it. That would have been so incredible to Ari. I wish that she could have known your name."

Gigi wiped the tears away before she continued. "I'd always called Ari bella from the time she was a baby. Well, you know that in Italian it means beautiful, and Arianna was always a beauty to me. But now you've come along and you're every bit as beautiful as your mother was. You are a Bella, my dear—true as your name."

Isabella didn't try to stop her tears as she cried openly, thoughts from weeks ago echoing in her mind.

Maybe she was a Bella.

She'd changed so much in the last few weeks. She could feel it —the shifting inside her of new ideas about who she was—new ideas of who she was becoming and what her future might hold.

Gigi reached across to squeeze her hand again. "Are you okay, honey? I'm sorry. I don't mean to overwhelm you."

"No. No, it's not that. Really. I love how honest you are with me about your thoughts and your feelings. I'm just trying to figure some things out for myself, you know? And I guess it is a little bit confusing, but I don't think it's bad—not really. Probably not unlike what a lot of people my age face, just different for me trying to process it all along with the information about my mother. I feel different, somehow, knowing so much more about her—about you all. It's like I've been given permission to be more of myself, if that makes sense."

Gigi smiled in response. "I think that makes perfect sense, and I also think that you are a very smart young woman. And for what it's worth, you have all of us here—I know I can speak on behalf of the others—cheering you on and ready to support you in any way that you need. We love you, Isabella. I love you. I want you to know that most of all when you leave here in a few days. We'll always be here for you. You've just inherited an extended family." She grinned and Isabella got up to come around the table and give her a big hug.

"I love you too, Gigi."

TWENTY-SEVEN

Isabella sat writing in her journal on the small sofa in her room. She had a perfect view out the window that overlooked the whole vineyard and she felt completely inspired as she expressed her thoughts and feelings on paper without effort.

She looked up in response to a light knock on the door.

"Come in."

"Hi. Am I interrupting anything?" Lia asked, opening the door enough to pop her head in.

"No. Not at all."

Isabella closed her journal, setting it on the small table next to her, and moved over on the sofa so that Lia could sit beside her.

She saw Lia's eyes go to her journal.

"You keep a journal?"

"Yeah. I've been writing in one since I was a little girl. It's helped, I guess—when things in my life have been pretty hectic. Believe it or not, I haven't always been this chilled out." Isabella laughed because she knew what an understatement this was. "What's this?"

Lia had placed an interesting-looking leather box on the coffee table in front of them. She reached over to pick up the box and set it on her lap. "Your mother bought this when we were together in Italy—in Florence, at the market those first days. It wasn't until the end—until her last days—that she told me what it was for and how special it was to her."

Isabella nodded, feeling curious to see what was inside. She noticed Lia wiping her eyes with a quick swipe of her hands, and then Lia reached over to take both of Isabella's hands in her own.

"My darling Isabella, I knew this day would come. I didn't know when but I knew that one day I'd be able to honor Ari's dying wish to be sure that you understood how much she loved you—that she'd thought about you every day and that her deepest regret was that she'd never know you as the young woman that you are today."

Isabella's heart was pounding and her own tears were starting to fall as she nodded her head, listening intently to her grandmother and watching as Lia reached down to pull off the lid of the box in her lap.

"These are the things that Ari wanted you to have." She pulled out a small tightly wrapped object and laid it in front of them on the table. "Ari wanted to be cremated and the majority of her ashes were spread in San Francisco. We had a little memorial for her there and let her ashes fall from the Golden Gate Bridge that she loved so much. But she had chosen two small urns—one for me and the other for you. This one is yours."

Isabella picked up the object from the table, not knowing whether she should be mortified or pleased that her mother would think that she wanted this to remember her by. Lia seemed to sense her confusion.

"Ari didn't have any specific expectations for what we should do with them. I keep mine on the mantle, but for the first year after she died, I kept it tucked away in my closet. You could spread them somewhere yourself if that made more sense to you."

Isabella nodded and set the urn back on the table. It was all a bit overwhelming all of a sudden, thinking that her mother's ashes were sitting right there in front of her.

"So, let's look at something a little less shocking maybe. Are you okay?" Lia leaned over and gave Isabella a quick hug. "Do you want to do this now?"

Isabella nodded. She was curious to see what else was in the box now.

Lia pulled a small envelope out and tilted it until a silver piece of jewelry landed in the palm of her hand. She stretched it out so that Isabella could see that it was a locket. She opened it to reveal a small picture of a dark-haired infant.

Isabella's eyes instantly filled with tears. "Is it—is that me?"

Lia was nodding her head. "It is."

Isabella took the bracelet out of Lia's hand and brought it nearer where she could study the infant in the picture. "Did Ari—did my mother hold me when I was born?" Her words felt choked as she struggled to get them out through the emotion she was feeling.

Lia reached out to stroke Isabella's hair, and she looked like she was barely managing to hold back her own tears as she spoke. "She did, bella. She held you on her chest for a few seconds after you were born. She saw how beautiful you were. She never forgot how you looked that day—not for one second."

Isabella nodded her head and swiped at her tears with her hand. She set the bracelet down on the table next to the urn and took a deep breath in, waiting because she knew that Lia had more to share with her.

Lia pulled what looked like a picture album from the box. It was big enough that it just fit within the sides of the space that contained it. "This was your mother's modeling book."

"My mother was a model?" She was surprised that no one had told her this about Arianna, although it certainly wasn't surprising because she was so beautiful.

"She was, yes. She was discovered as a teen-ager by an agent and did mostly print work up until the time of her parent's accident. But actually, it's not her modeling pictures that are in this book." Lia opened it to the first page which, showed a single shot of Arianna making a goofy face—the first of many selfies that she'd taken during those last few months of her life.

Isabella smiled and took the album into her lap as she turned the page.

"She didn't like her modeling pics at the end. She said one time that they were all fake—not the real her at all—and she wanted you to see her as she was during those last months—before she was so sick..." Lia's voice trailed off, and Isabella didn't miss how hard it might be for Lia as they looked at these pictures—many of which were taken during their time spent together in Italy.

Isabella reached over to take her grandmother's hand as she turned the page to see a picture of Lia and Ari together, the wind blowing their hair, both of their faces in wide grins as they smiled for the camera.

And there was picture after picture of Arianna looking happy and healthy, some with the others—Blu, Jemma, Gigi and Lia—and some just of herself—in her convertible, walking across the Golden Gate Bridge, sitting in the garden that Lia said she loved so much. All of these pictures helped Isabella to feel just that much closer to her, like she was glimpsing just a little bit more of who her mother was—of the woman who had desperately wanted Isabella to know her.

Isabella wiped at her eyes, taking a deep breath in, knowing there were still a few items in the box. This was more difficult than she'd imagined it would be, but it was why she'd come here—to learn everything she could about her mother. And she felt Arianna's presence and her intentions in the careful assembly of these things that she'd put together for a daughter that she'd never know.

She looked up when she heard a quiet knock at the half-opened door. She smiled when she saw Gigi and Blu, with Jemma right behind them. "Come in."

"We're interrupting," Blu said when she glanced over to see what Isabella and Lia were looking at.

"Yes, we can come back," Gigi said, turning to leave.

"No, no. Stay. I don't mind." Isabella turned to Lia. "If it's okay with you?"

"This is all about you, sweet girl." Lia leaned over to give her a kiss on the cheek."

The women walked in the room nearer to the little sitting area, Gigi and Blu taking seats on the remaining two chairs and Jemma folding her legs underneath her as she sat down near where Isabella sat on the sofa.

"Oh, the box," Jemma, said smiling. "All of the mysteries of the box."

Lia laughed lightly. "Honey, you were too young to understand what all of this meant back then."

"Oh, I know. I'm totally happy for you, girl. It's exciting." Jemma reached up to give Isabella a big hug.

The hug and the emotions behind it were true and sweet and it caught Isabella by surprise. Ever since she'd gotten here, being with these women had made her feel special, like she was part of a secret club—a club that she fit into easily, just because of the person that she was.

Jemma was peering into the box. "So what's left?" She winked.

Lia pulled out several books, some of which were nicer—with leather covers—and some of which looked like plain notebooks that one would buy for school. She placed them on the table and all the women stared at them. "You should read these later—probably when you're alone. We've never read them. They're just for you."

The other women were nodding their heads in agreement and sharing in the knowledge that they understood exactly what these hundreds of pieces of paper represented.

"What—what is this—what are they?" Isabella reached out to slide her fingers across the worn leather cover of the book that lay on top of the pile. Her heart beat faster. She thought she understood but she couldn't be sure until she opened the first cover to peak inside. "My mother kept a journal?"

Gigi was nodding her head. "That girl wrote in her journal nearly every day. It was one of her most favorite things to do. She said that it relaxed her."

Lia was nodding. "She was a great writer, actually. We've got some of her short stories, and you can read those too." She pulled out one of the leather journals near the top of the pile. "This one is special. She told me to have you read the blue one first."

Isabella didn't bother to try to stop the tears as they made their way down her face. Her mother was a writer—just like her. It was overwhelming to her—that she was going to be able to read all of these pages of emotions and feelings that had poured out of her mother over the course of her life.

"This is all so incredible, isn't it? I mean, I can't believe that she did this for me."

"Bella, Ari would have done anything for you. She loved you very much," Gigi said.

"During her final time with us, she made each of us promise that you would know that about her—that you would know how much she loved you—how much she wanted for you to be happy," said Lia, hugging Isabella close. "It's so wonderful that we finally have that opportunity with you—and that we get a chance to love you too."

Isabella was feeling emotionally drained as she stacked up the journals on the table next to the other items.

Jemma sat forward to peer into the box still on the sofa between Isabella and Lia. "There's something else in there." She reached in to take out a large folded paper and handed it to Isabella.

"What's this?"

Lia was moving everything from the table in front of them back into the box.

"Unfold it—here on the table."

TWENTY-EIGHT

Gigi moved around to help Isabella unfold what looked like a large piece of paper out onto the coffee table. "It's the map," she said.

"What map?"

"Ari's map." Gigi smoothed it out across the table with her hand, a funny look on her face. "She used to sit with it spread out on the floor of her room, planning this magnificent trip—the trip of a lifetime, she called it."

It was a world map, dotted with marker, stickers and little notes. Isabella smiled when she saw that the Tuscany region of Italy had a gold star with the words "start here" written in Arianna's handwriting.

She thought about her own stash of travel books back home in her closet and how she'd spent hours poring over them planning her own trip of a lifetime—a trip that had always had a slim chance of actually happening for so many different reasons.

Jemma put her head close to Isabella's as they looked over the areas marked—there were several countries marked throughout Europe besides Italy—Portugal, Spain, Germany and Greece. There were marks for several spots throughout Asia, Australia, New Zealand, Central and South America.

"Was she planning a trip around the world?" Isabella directed her question toward Gigi, who seemed to know the most about the map.

"Yes, she was. Her father's travel agent was helping her to plan it right before they were killed in the plane crash. It was Ari's graduation present from them." Gigi pulled a tissue out from her pocket and wiped at her eyes.

Isabella was reminded of all the devastation that Gigi had suffered with the loss of the entire Sinclair family. She reached over to take Gigi's hand as she continued to speak.

"Then when Ari found out she was dying, it was the only thing she wanted to do—to take this whirlwind trip around the world, which of course had us all worried to death." Gigi looked toward Blu, who was nodding her head.

"Yes, that was a difficult time—trying to be supportive of her wishes while at the same time thinking about her health, but there was no convincing her otherwise. Besides, it wasn't our place to say, really," said Blu. "Ari was gonna do whatever she wanted to do and she wanted to take this trip."

"Except, then she met me," Lia said.

"That's right." Gigi smiled. "And she never regretted the decision to do the trip with you here. She told me that it was the best time of her life."

They were all quiet and Isabella's thoughts and emotions were racing. She'd learned so much about her mother over the last few days. She never in a million years would have guessed that they would share such similar passions—and talents. It was hard to put into words, and she knew that it was something she had yet to process.

As she looked around at the women sitting next to her, all linked by a common love for the young woman who had meant so much to them and who had really changed their lives by what she'd given them, Isabella felt a part of it all—a part of them. And she did feel her mother's love for her. She knew that it was exactly the right time and exactly what her mother had hoped for.

Lia leaned in to give her a hug and kiss, and as if on cue, the others stood up.

"We'll leave you alone, honey. This is a lot to take in and I'm sure you'd like some time to yourself," said Lia.

Isabella nodded, picking up the blue journal from the stack on the table, holding it close to her chest.

"Thank you. I don't even know what to say about all this. I'm a little overwhelmed, to be honest. I'll come join you all in a little while."

Jemma stopped to give her another big hug before she walked out the door. "Take all the time you need."

Isabella returned to the small sofa with the blue journal still in her hands. Her heart pounding slightly faster than normal, she slowly folded the leather cover back to peek inside at the pages that her mother had wanted her to read first.

She felt her throat constrict and the forming of instant tears as she realized that she was looking at a letter from her mother.

TWENTY-NINE

My Dearest Daughter,

I'm so sorry that these words will never be spoken for you to hear them from my lips. I wanted so badly to meet you one day—to hold you in my arms finally for more than just the short seconds we had together the day that you were born.

I'm sorry that you might have unanswered questions. It was never my intention to not be able to share with you all the thoughts I've ever had about you ever since the day that you were born, but fate had something else in mind, so the words on this page and the words spoken by those closest to me will have to be enough. I pray that it will be.

Where to start...there's so much to say, isn't there?

I want you to know, most of all, that every day I've regretted that I didn't fight harder to keep you. I never wanted to give you up, but I think, given the circumstances, perhaps it has been the best thing for you after all. I've hoped and prayed every day that you've had a good life—that you've felt loved and that you've had everything you could need to be happy.

Your happiness is what drives me daily now as I watch the clock tick toward the end for me.

By the time you are reading this letter, you will have met everyone that has meant so much to me—Gigi—hopefully Douglas is still by her side—her husband if I've had any say in it. ;)

Isabella laughed out loud through her tears at Arianna, the matchmaker, at work.

—Lia (your grandmother), Blu and Jemma.

My greatest wish now is that you would know them all and be loved by them all the way that I was—and that they will have the chance to know you too.

I know you might be wondering about your father. I've not spoken a great deal about him to the others. I'm afraid that I've not been fair to him about any of this—your birth or my death. He loved me at one time and he deserved to know about you, but my parents wouldn't allow it while they were alive and—well, I'm sorry to say that I was a coward in that regard. But I think he'd want to know you, so I will leave that to you and in the back of this book, you'll find his name and the last known address and phone number that I have for him. Locating him is something that Douglas can probably help you with if that time should come—and why shouldn't it? You deserve to know the full truth of who you are, my sweet girl.

Her father. Isabella had asked Douglas about it during one of their earliest conversations and he'd said that, sadly, it wasn't something that Arianna had ever really talked to him about. She turned to the last page of the journal, running her fingers over the name and information that might one day lead her to her birth father. It was another piece of the puzzle—this time given to her by her mother.

She took a deep breath and turned back toward the front of the journal to continue reading the letter.

By now, Douglas will have told you about the trust that I've set up for you and all about the wealth that I'd grown up with. None of it ever really meant that much to me except I know that it bought me some opportunities in life that I might not have known otherwise. It definitely bought me some special experiences with Lia and with the others—those are the things that have meant the most to me during these last days.

I want you to use the money for your education if that's your wish or your need, but you have my blessing to use it for your dreams— whatever those might be—and truly there is plenty there for everything you could ever want for. I love that I can give that to you now and I only wish that I could be there to share in it all with you.

Isabella thought about all of her mom's journals she had yet to read and the map that was tucked into the box of things that Arianna had wanted her to have. It was as if that little box held every bit of confirmation that she'd never even realized she could seek about what she'd always known in her heart—about her own dreams to be a writer and maybe even travel the world one day. She flashed back to the question that Jemma had asked her just days ago—was she a lawyer or a writer?

Isabella felt a settling in her heart as she turned her attention back to the letter. In this moment, she knew exactly who she was.

Do what you like with the things in the box. My intention with each item is that they would help you to have a better sense of who I was and what my dreams were as a young girl. But don't spend one moment worrying about me now. I've come to a total peace about my life and my death. I've forgiven myself even for the decisions made that took you from me. It is only about moving forward now, and this letter to you is a part of all that for me, just as I hope that it will be for you too.

Gigi called me bella ever since I was a small child. I remember asking her why she called me that one time. (And I bet that she is calling you bella now too.) She told me that it meant beautiful and that I was beautiful, but not only on the outside. She said that it was her term for me for all the beauty I possessed inside—some of it yet to be brought out into the world.

So, my dearest daughter, I shall call you Bella—for I know that you are a true beauty, inside and out—preparing to live a life that is full of love and happiness.

That's my wish for you, my sweet Bella.

I love you more than you could ever know.

Your Mother,
  Arianna Sinclair

Isabella closed the journal and held it tightly to her chest as she sobbed. Her tears were not of sadness, but of hope for a future that had now shifted for her. With these final words from her mother came a sense of direction unlike any she'd known before in her young lifetime.

She smiled as she thought about the decisions to be made in the next few days. She *was* a Bella. She knew that now.

THIRTY

Isabella knocked lightly on the door to Antonio's office, where Gigi had sent her to talk to Douglas. She'd come downstairs and spoken with her grandparents first, about her plans and to get their blessing, which she'd felt confident that she'd have. Now she was counting on Douglas to be on board for helping her with the logistics of everything that needed to happen. She was confident about his help also, something that made her smile—that she felt she had so much support from a small group of people that she hadn't even known a month ago.

"Come in."

She heard Douglas's voice from the other side of the door.

"Hi." She poked her head in the door. "Do you have a few minutes?"

"Of course. Come in." He smiled as he took off his glasses and closed his laptop. He gestured toward the chair opposite him across the desk. "Have a seat. What's on your mind?"

"Well..." She grinned at him, feeling excited to tell him about the decisions she'd made.

"Yes?" He grinned back. "You look like someone who has really good news."

Isabella nodded. "I do, yes. I've just come from speaking with my grandparents about staying on a bit longer."

"Oh, yeah? That's great, Isabella."

"Thanks." She loved that she felt he was genuinely happy to hear the news. "So I was wondering if you could help me with something."

"I'm sure that I'd be happy to. What do you need?"

"Well, I think that you said everything about the trust has been set up now; is that right?"

"Yes, that's right. It's all there in your account now ready for you to use."

"Okay, great. I want to fly my parents out as soon as possible. Well, I still need to talk to them but my grandparents have said that they'd love to have them here."

"That's wonderful. I'm sure that they're quite welcome. It will be great for the others to meet the people responsible for the lovely woman you've turned out to be."

"Thanks. Can you help me with the tickets? I'd like to fly them first class." Isabella was beyond excited because she knew that it was just the beginning of what would be many plane tickets she'd be purchasing very soon, and also the first of many things she planned to do for her parents.

"Of course. I'll call the travel agent that we use here. Just let me know when you're ready."

"Also..."

Isabella felt oddly fine asking the question that would have seemed crazy even a month ago.

"Yes, what it is, my dear?"

"Well, this seems a little frivolous but I'm trying to adjust to this idea that I can actually splurge a little bit."

Douglas smiled, instantly putting her at ease. "Of course you can. Your mom would have wanted that. I promise you that."

"Okay. So, I'd like to rent a convertible for while I'm here."

"Say no more. I know just the place and can have one over here for you in the morning."

"Perfect. Thanks, Douglas."

He nodded his head.

"For everything, I mean. It's clear to me that you meant a great deal to my mother and I want to be sure that you know how much everything you're doing—how much you and everyone mean to me."

Douglas got up to come around the desk and Isabella stood to give him a big hug.

"Well, you mean everything to us also. It's completely my pleasure to help you with anything you need. Gigi and I will be heading back to the orphanage soon, but we're always only a phone call or a text away. And you must come visit us. We'd love to have you and I think you'd like it there. The children will adore you."

Isabella loved it when Douglas spoke about the kids and the orphanage. His face seemed to light up and there was a certain energy about the way he talked that made her want to see more into this little world that he and Gigi talked so much about.

"I'd love to come. And I am definitely adding that to my list of places to visit." She winked at Douglas.

"Oh, so there's a list now, is there?" He laughed.

"Oh, there's a list alright."

THIRTY-ONE

Isabella had excused herself after a very festive dinner. Everyone was very pleased to hear that she was staying on for at least a few more weeks. She hadn't even had a chance yet to talk to Jemma about her real plans, and she was anxious to hear her thoughts about everything that had been on her mind. They'd made a lunch plan for the next day, and by then Isabella thought that she might have an even clearer picture of how the next few months were going to go.

There were two things that she needed to do before she moved forward with her plans. She'd already e-mailed Ms. Carlson, and she felt confident enough now to call her parents.

She took a deep breath before pulling up the number on her phone, recognizing that she still felt slightly nervous even though she was sure about her decision. She did notice, though, that throughout her decision-making process, she'd not felt that anxious upset stomach at all—not for one second. She took this as a sign that everything she was doing was exactly the right thing for her. And she reminded herself that everything was going to be new for her parents. The daughter calling them now was not exactly the same daughter that had left them over a week ago.

"Hello? Iz? Is that you, honey?" It was her father's phone that she'd called, and hearing his voice in her ear made her smile.

"Hi, Dad. Is Mom there too? I miss you guys."

"We miss you too, honey. Yes, let me get Mom—one sec."

She heard him call for her and seconds later, sounding slightly breathless, her Mom was on the phone too.

"Honey, we've got you on speaker phone. Oh, it's so good to hear your voice. We miss you and can't wait for you to come home."

Isabella wouldn't let the words deter her from the message that she needed to deliver.

"I miss you guys too. Really. But that's some of what I want to talk to you about."

She felt a quick pang of something slight but reminiscent of the anxiety that she knew well. She took another deep breath and willed it away.

Just be honest, Isabella.

And she smiled. What she was doing was good. It was the right thing for her. She was sure of that.

"Go on, honey. But you're making me feel nervous to hear what you're going to say," her mother said.

"Don't be nervous, just please hear me out, okay?"

"Okay, Izzy. Go ahead," her father said.

"I've decided to stay here in Italy longer, but I want to fly you guys out. Lia and Antonio—and everyone here—want to meet you, and you can stay here at the villa. And the cost is no problem. Douglas made sure that the trust is all lined up now and before you say no, just please let me tell you everything." Isabella stopped to catch her breath, and the silence that followed for several seconds was deafening to her.

Please understand.

"Iz, how long are you talking about staying?"

It was her mom asking the question and Isabella definitely detected something in her voice—fear, maybe.

"Well, I need to tell you guys that I've decided to defer my enrollment at Harvard. I've asked Ms. Carlson, my high school guidance counselor, to help me with everything, but from what I can see, it shouldn't be a problem."

She thought that this was the best way to break the news to them, but deep down she didn't know if it was true that she'd ever be attending Harvard. She knew about not closing doors though, so deferment was the obvious best choice anyway—until she had more of an idea of what her year was going to look like.

"Honey, are you sure that's what you want? What are you going to do for the year?" her father asked.

"I have some ideas, but really, Dad, I'd love to be able to share that all with you guys in person. Please say that you'll come for the visit. I can get you on a flight as early as next week. I know it's late notice but if you can make it work with your schedules—really, I need to talk to you about work. Maybe you guys don't even need to be working so hard now—now that I have all this money just sitting in my bank account and—"

"Isabella, don't even talk like that. It's your money." Her mother was quick to interrupt her, and Isabella wasn't surprised that they'd have strong feelings about what she should and shouldn't do with the money.

"Mom, it's a lot of money. You know that it is. More than I could ever spend, really. But we'll talk more about it. Right now, I just—I really miss you both. I want to do something nice for you and I want to see you. And I just know that you're going to love it here. I'm sorry. I know it might seem kind of weird to meet everyone but I really think that everything will be fine—more than fine."

There was silence again on the other end of the line and then Isabella could make out the whispers between her parents.

"Honey, we'd love to come see you. Of course we will. But we can get our tickets. Don't worry about that," her father said.

"No, really, Dad. I think they'll be expensive to get them last-minute like this and I—just let me get them please. I want to do this for you."

More whispers, and then it was her mom's voice. "Okay, honey. Sure. And I can't wait to see you—and Italy for the first time."

They continued to talk about the upcoming trip, and finally Isabella heard excitement in their voices. She was actually shocked at how well her news about deferring school had gone over, even though she knew that there would still be more discussions to come about that. They promised to take care of getting the time off work right away, and Isabella said she'd be sending them the details for the tickets within the next day or two.

This was a big hurdle overcome—maybe one of the biggest for her.

THIRTY-TWO

Jemma talked a mile a minute when she was excited, and Isabella especially loved this about her new friend. They settled in at the outside table of the little trattoria and ordered their pizzas, Isabella excited to share more of her plans.

"Bella—so can I call you that? Or no? Sorry. Just tell me."

Isabella laughed. The nickname still felt a little strange but she'd decided that it was something that she was going to officially accept.

During the drive over, she'd told Jemma about the letter, not leaving anything out. It wasn't necessarily usual for her to share something so personal, but she trusted Jemma completely. She'd shared a lot with her new friend over the past few days.

"Yes, you can call me what you like." Isabella was really enjoying the easy banter that they'd seemed to develop so early in their friendship.

"So, I can't wait to hear what you're thinking. Tell me everything."

Isabella laughed and thought about where she should start. After she'd spoken with her parents the night before, she'd received a very enthusiastic e-mail back from Ms. Carlson assuring her that she'd be able to help her take care of the deferment request. Ms. Carlson had written that she was proud of Isabella for making the decisions that she'd made and absolutely ecstatic about the plans that Isabella had described to her.

Isabella pulled Arianna's folded map out from the large tote bag beside her and laid it on the table.

"So, there's something that I've not shared with you yet. It's something I've only really shared with Thomas."

Isabella had told Jemma all about her best friend back home, already anxious for the day that he and Jemma would meet.

"Oh, do tell." Jemma grinned as she took a sip of her coffee and settled back into her chair.

"For as long as I can remember, I've had these big travel dreams, collecting ridiculous numbers of travel books that it seemed I'd never use." She noticed the question on Jemma's face. "I mean, just ridiculous in the sense that they've been sitting in my closet, and for whatever reason I seemed to have this intense fear of flying."

"A fear that you've overcome." Jemma grinned.

"Exactly." Isabella smiled and looked down at the folded map she'd laid on the table in front of them. She folded back the side that showed what Arianna had marked off in Europe. "So, now that I've fully embraced this idea that my mother left me this vast amount of money, I've been thinking more about my future and what I might really want. The thing is, Jemma—I honestly don't know if I want to become a lawyer. It feels kind of weird to say that because it's all that I've told myself for so many years."

Jemma was nodding her head, and everything on her face told Isabella that she was one hundred percent getting exactly what Isabella was saying.

"Jemma, what if I take this journey that Arianna—that my mother—never got to take?"

Isabella couldn't stop the tears from coming. From the moment she'd unfolded the map and realized what it was—realized that she and her mother had shared this same dream to travel the world—she knew that she would do it.

She'd take this magnificent trip of a lifetime, not only for herself, but for Arianna. When she'd read her mother's wishes for her in the letter, she knew that it was the one thing that she could do to honor those wishes and honor the memory of a mother who'd loved her so much.

Jemma's eyes were teary now too as she listened to Isabella and watched her cry.

Finally Isabella wiped away the last of her tears, ready to focus on the other point of the conversation that she'd wanted to have with Jemma. "You've mentioned that you want to travel too, and I just thought that maybe this would be something cool we could do together—something I think my mom would have really loved. Jemma, do you want to join me?"

She watched her friend's face in anticipation as Jemma's grin only got wider.

Jemma laughed. "It's as if you read my mind. I had the exact same thought when we were looking at the map the other day, but I didn't want to assume anything—and I had no idea if you really wanted to travel. I've been thinking about a trip."

"You have?"

"I've been so inspired painting here in Tuscany. I've imagined how it might be to travel and just focus on my art."

"And I've been having the same thoughts about—"

"—Your writing!" Jemma interrupted. "Oh, I bet you'd be so inspired. We have to do this, Iz. Yes, I'm so down with this idea."

They both laughed, and Isabella had the thought again of how lucky she was to have these new people in her life who had so quickly become her friends.

"There's so many places I want to see, including everything my mother had already mapped out, and of course you can add to that list as well. And we can always start with Europe as sort of a test— and just go from there."

Jemma was nodding her head

"We're gonna have a lot of fun planning this, aren't we, Jem?"

Jemma laughed. "I can't wait. Oh, and we can meet up with Thomas if you want. I'm sure he's gonna freak out when you tell him your plans."

"That's for sure. I wanted to talk to you first, but yeah, he's gonna be beside himself."

They ate their lunch and then spent hours poring over the map and adding places to the list in the notebook of ideas that Isabella had already started.

THIRTY-THREE

Isabella stopped just inside the doorway to the outside patio, not yet noticed by everyone seated around the big table. It was their last dinner all together before her parents left in the morning.

Emily and Richard had been able to get away from work for a week and the time had gone way too fast. Isabella had been right in her decision to invite them, and as she'd anticipated, her parents seemed just as taken with everyone as Isabella had been. It had been fun touring Tuscany with them and they'd also made a quick trip to Florence and the coast.

Isabella loved watching them all interact—this extended family that she'd inherited.

Her parents sat next to Lia and Antonio at one end of the table, her mom's and Lia's heads close together looking at what Isabella guessed were pictures on her mother's phone.

Douglas was so sweet with Gigi. Isabella smiled as he pulled her down on his lap while she seemed to be attempting to make her way back toward the kitchen.

Blu and Chase were deeply involved with whatever Jemma was showing them on her sketchpad, and Gabriela and Kylie were giggling as they put away their card game at the other end of the table.

Isabella felt that if she stood there one more moment looking at the scene in front of her, her heart would burst from contentment. She'd never imagined a time in her life when she'd feel this complete or this sure of herself.

Lia looked up and her eyes connected with Isabella's. "There she is. Come sit here with us." She scooted over so that Isabella could sit between her and Emily. "Dinner's ready."

Isabella made her way over and sat down.

"Honey, I was just showing Lia the pictures from our trip."

Isabella leaned over to kiss her mom on the cheek. "You got some really good shots during the drive, Mom."

Her mother nodded. "Your father and I are jealous of all the gorgeous scenery you have in your near future."

"And slightly nervous to think about you girls driving here on your—"

"Dad." Isabella interrupted him, the tone of her voice stern, but she was smiling. "You know we're going to be fine. Jemma and I are both excellent drivers."

Jemma grinned from across the table when she heard her name. "Don't worry, Mr. Dawson. We're going to take great care of one another."

"We're not worried," Isabella's mother said. "Well, okay. Maybe just slightly worried, but I know you kids will be fine."

Isabella had told her parents her full plan the day after they'd arrived in Italy, and she'd been completely shocked at how well they'd handled everything. The support that they were giving her about her plans to travel and write was beyond any best-case scenario that she could have imagined. They loved it that she and Jemma would be traveling together, rather than Isabella being on her own, especially after they'd now spent some time with Jemma.

All eyes went toward Antonio as he stood up at the head of the table to lift his glass of wine in a toast.

"To the Dawsons—Emily, Richard, and our darling Isabella. May this be the first of many wonderful times that we spend together. It's been wonderful having you in our home, which we would love for you to consider as your home now too."

"Cheers," rang out from around the table.

Everyone raised their glasses, and Isabella's father was the next to speak.

"Thank you for having us—and for making this time so special for us—but more importantly for making it so special for Isabella —for welcoming her into your families and your lives."

Isabella was nodding, tears streaming down her face.

The days after Isabella's parents left passed quickly. Douglas had had to get back to the orphanage, but Gigi had decided to stay for a few days longer to see Isabella and Jemma off on the first leg of their trip.

They'd spend one month driving to the south of Italy, stopping wherever inspiration led them, before flying to London, where they were planning to meet up with Thomas.

With the convertible packed and ready to go they'd enjoyed one last big lunch at Thyme and now it was time to say goodbye. Isabella's emotions were all over the place as she hugged and kissed everyone goodbye. Everything that had happened over the last month had been life-changing for her, and she knew now beyond a shadow of a doubt that her trip to Italy was only the very tip of the iceberg of what her life was going to become—of the ways that she was going to honor Arianna—honor her mother—by living out her own dreams.

Isabella sat down in the driver's seat of the convertible and tucked Arianna's folded map in between the two seats. She pulled out her phone and plugged in the cord that would play their music through the car's speaker system. Isabella showed the *La Boheme* soundtrack to Jemma, who nodded her head in agreement; and with one look and wave over their shoulders, they were finally off.

Isabella glanced in the rearview mirror and had to swipe away her own tears as she saw Gigi and Blu close together watching them still from the restaurant.

Jemma was smiling, but looked somber. "We must look like them—like our mothers did driving down the road together in Arianna's car."

Isabella nodded, wiping at her eyes as she noticed that her mother's map, that she'd placed in between them, was now lying on the floor at her feet. As they pulled up to a stop sign, she reached down to get it and handed it to Jemma.

"Will you tuck this somewhere safe please?"

Jemma took it in her hand and was about to open the glove compartment when she brought the map close to her face.

"Iz, pull over."

"What? What is it?" Isabella obeyed without asking questions.

"Did you see this note on the back of the map? It's so faint that I can barely make it out."

Isabella reached for the paper, squinting her eyes a bit to make out the faint writing that Jemma was pointing to.

"It's there. Right in the corner."

A map for Bella...Enjoy the journey!

Isabella swallowed the lump in her throat and managed to hold the tears back this time. She handed the map back to Jemma as she started the car again.

Jemma shut the glove box after placing the map inside and reached for the volume on the stereo dial. "Are you ready, Bella?"

Isabella nodded and grinned as she pulled onto the road with the first loud chords of the opera music filling the space around them in the car.

"Let the journey begin!"

THE STORY CONTINUES

Bella's Hope
Legacy Series, Book 7

Available on Amazon

PaulaKayBooks.com

BELLA'S HOPE — PREVIEW

Chapter 1

Isabella Dawson looked up from her laptop, aware of her friend's presence as Jemma stared intently at her from the doorway.

"You look great, Jem. Hot date?"

"No. No date. Just going out with the girls we met at the cafe yesterday." Jemma seemed to be eyeing her carefully before she continued. "Come with us, Bella. Seriously, you've been working nonstop and—"

"I can't." Isabella cut her friend off. "You know how close I am to finishing."

Jemma was nodding her head, but it was an argument the two had been having more and more, lately, during their travels.

"I know. I know, but Bella—it's Paris." Jemma gestured toward the window where they had the most stunning view of the Eiffel Tower.

Isabella took in a deep breath. If she was being honest with herself, she knew that she'd become more than a bit obsessed with finishing her book. Despite the changing landscape outside their rented apartments, finishing the book seemed to be all she thought about these days—well, that and the much anticipated upcoming meeting with her birth father, Lucas. The sudden thought made her heart pound faster.

"I know. You're probably right, but I'm just having a hard time relaxing—thinking about the deadline and—and everything."

"Your self-imposed deadline, you mean."

Isabella felt her face go hot. She'd come a long way since high school—since her trip to Italy only months ago—but shaking her perfectionist tendencies was proving harder than she'd anticipated.

"Yeah, I know. What can I say?" She laughed lightly, willing her friend to understand.

True to form, Jemma crossed the room to put her arms around Isabella, giving her a quick kiss on top of her head. "I know. I get it. And you're right. It is important. I know you want to publish it before Christmas. I'm cheering you on—promise."

The two hugged and Isabella thought about how lucky she was—for about the millionth time since she and Jemma had begun their European journey together, months earlier. She and Jemma were so different in many ways—Jemma was definitely the free spirit of the two—but somehow they'd made an unbelievable connection and now Isabella couldn't imagine her life without her new best friend.

"You're a great cheerleader. It means a lot to me. Truly. And I'm actually hoping to be done before London—before we meet Thomas. If I can get the rough draft done in the next week or so, I'll be able to enjoy England and Ireland with you guys. Besides, Thomas would kill me if I spent this much time on my computer when we're finally getting together."

"Well, I can't wait to meet Thomas finally. You guys have talked so much during our trip that I feel like I already know him."

"The video chats have been fun, huh?" No matter how busy things had gotten, Isabella had honored her weekly video chat commitment with both Thomas and her parents back in Connecticut.

"Very fun—especially given how cute that so-called *best friend* of yours is." Jemma winked at her and Isabella laughed in response.

"I'm not sure what I need to do to convince you. Thomas and I are *just* friends. You'll see that when you meet him. He's practically like a brother to me."

"So then you don't care that I find him extremely attractive?"

Jemma was teasing her, but there was no denying the instant feeling the thought caused in Isabella's gut. She didn't know exactly why, but the thought of Thomas liking Jemma in a romantic way caused her stress. Well, they were her two best friends, and potential friction between them wouldn't be good. Isabella hadn't been in many relationships herself, but she knew enough about Thomas's track record to know that his relationships—at least thus far—had known their share of friction.

"Bella." Jemma's nudge brought Isabella out of her thoughts. "You know I'm only joking."

"Well, I'm not sure about Thomas being the right guy for you but I do know that you deserve someone great, Jem."

"As do you." Jemma walked across the room to pick up her handbag from the table. "But neither of us are really looking for relationships on this trip, now are we?" Jemma laughed. "Might I remind you of our pact?"

When they'd started their European adventure a few months earlier, they'd discussed at length their goals for the trip. Besides their mutual desire to explore their creative ideas—Jemma with her painting and Isabella with her writing—they both felt that it was the perfect time in their lives to be selfish, learning more about themselves and what they wanted to do after their big adventure.

And Isabella had the journal from Arianna—the greatest gift that her birth mother had left her when she died. The letters that she'd written to Isabella in that leather-bound book had meant more to Isabella than anything else she held in her possession. She'd not shared those private letters with anyone yet—not even Jemma. Even as she had the quick thought, Isabella knew that the journey she was on was to be shaped not only by the map that Arianna had left her, but by those words her mother had written just for her.

"Hello. Earth to Bella." Jemma's voice interrupted Isabella's thoughts.

"Oh, sorry. Right. The pact." She smiled at her friend as she got up from the desk in the corner of the living room. "We've got plenty of time for boyfriends, right?"

"And plenty of time to just have a little fun. And on that note —don't wait up."

"Jem, be careful, okay?"

"As always." Jemma turned to smile at her as she opened the door. "And if you change your mind, text me."

"Will do. Have fun."

Chapter 2

Isabella closed her laptop and crossed the room to the kitchen to put the teakettle on. She'd gotten into the ritual of having tea during her nighttime writing sessions ever since they'd arrived in Paris three weeks earlier. She sat down at the small table in the breakfast nook to wait for the water to boil.

When she and Jemma had found the apartment rental online, they'd both fallen in love with it instantly. The place had big windows and wonderful little balconies—all of which revealed the stunning views of the Eiffel Tower and the beautiful city below. Isabella felt like pinching herself yet again as she stared out the window.

She'd never in her wildest dreams imagined that she'd be on this trip of a lifetime to begin with, let alone able to afford the luxury accommodations that they'd been able to rent along the way. She hadn't grown up like that. She was only just starting to understand what it felt like to not have financial concerns—to have the ability to say yes to anything, regardless of the price tag.

And she and Jemma had been saying yes to a lot when it came to their travels. They'd already extended the first part of their trip to include much of France, which was how they'd come to be in Paris. They were both enjoying the inspiration that they'd felt while in Italy and France. Isabella's writing had accelerated and Jemma had painted some of the most beautiful pieces of her life thus far.

They hadn't quite been ready to head to London upon Thomas's arrival there a month earlier, and when Isabella had invited him to join them in Paris, he'd declined. Finally, after much prodding, he'd admitted to the fact that he was quite enamored with a woman he'd met—someone he'd been chatting with online before arriving in London. Isabella couldn't help but roll her eyes as she even thought about the conversation that they'd had about her. He'd even used the word enamored, which had totally thrown her for a loop. She knew that Thomas was probably just having some fun and she'd get the real scoop from him soon enough.

Isabella got up to walk over to the map that they'd tacked up on the wall—Arianna's map—her birth mother's map from so long ago. She used to tear up whenever she'd look at it, but now those tears had been replaced with a fierce determination to make this trip count—to see everything that the young Arianna had never been able to see before she'd died.

Even as she had the thought, it made her feel uncomfortable. Jemma would probably tell a different story. She'd expressed her fears that Isabella was missing out on so much—staying in writing during so many of the days spent in gorgeous European cities. But Jemma hadn't read the letters.

The whistle of the teakettle interrupted Isabella's thoughts. She made her cup of tea and walked back into the living room, placing it on the end table while she went to her bedroom to retrieve the journal. She'd been keeping a journal herself during the trip—just as she'd always done—but tonight she needed to reread the letters from her mother. She needed some fortification for the choices she was making—for the anguish that she was feeling about finishing her book.

She sat back on the comfy sofa and opened the worn leather cover to the pages she'd read more times than she could count since the book had been placed in her hands only a few months earlier. She knew the words by heart, yet she loved to look at her mother's handwriting—she felt connected to her when she read them, something that she knew Arianna had wanted desperately for her daughter.

My Dearest Daughter,

I'm so sorry that these words will never be spoken for you to hear them from my lips. I wanted so badly to meet you one day—to hold you in my arms finally for more than just the short seconds we had together the day that you were born.

I'm sorry that you might have unanswered questions. It was never my intention to not be able to share with you all the thoughts I've ever had about you ever since the day that you were born, but fate had something else in mind, so the words on this page and the words spoken by those closest to me will have to be enough. I pray that it will be.

Where to start...there's so much to say, isn't there?

I want you to know, most of all, that every day I've regretted that I didn't fight harder to keep you. I never wanted to give you up, but I think, given the circumstances, perhaps it has been the best thing for you after all. I've hoped and prayed every day that you've had a good life—that you've felt loved and that you've had everything you could need to be happy.

Your happiness is what drives me daily now as I watch the clock tick toward the end for me.

By the time you are reading this letter, you will have met everyone that has meant so much to me: Gigi—hopefully Douglas is still by her side; her husband if I've had any say in it ;)—Lia (your grandmother), Blu, and Jemma.

My greatest wish now is that you would know them all and be loved by them all in the way that I was—and that they will have the chance to know you too.

I know you might be wondering about your father. I've not spoken a great deal about him to the others. I'm afraid that I've not been fair to him about any of this—your birth or my death. He loved me at one time and he deserved to know about you, but my parents wouldn't allow it while they were alive and—well, I'm sorry to say that I was a coward in that regard. But I think he'd want to know you, so I will leave that to you and in the back of this book, you'll find his name and the last known address and phone number that I have for him. Locating him is something that Douglas can probably help you with if that time should come—and why shouldn't it? You deserve to know the full truth of who you are, my sweet girl.

By now, Douglas will have told you about the trust that I've set up for you and all about the wealth that I'd grown up with. None of it ever really meant that much to me, except I know that it bought me some opportunities in life that I might not have known otherwise. It definitely bought me some special experiences with Lia and with the others—those are the things that have meant the most to me during these last days.

I want you to use the money for your education if that's your wish or your need, but you have my blessing to use it for your dreams— whatever those might be—and truly there is plenty there for everything you could ever want for. I love that I can give that to you now and I only wish that I could be there to share in it all with you.

Do what you like with the things in the box. My intention with each item is that they would help you to have a better sense of who I was and what my dreams were as a young girl. But don't spend one moment worrying about me now. I've come to a total peace about my life and my death. I've forgiven myself even for the decisions made that took you from me. It is only about moving forward now, and this letter to you is a part of all that for me, just as I hope that it will be for you too.

Gigi called me bella ever since I was a small child. I remember asking her why she called me that one time. (And I bet that she is calling you bella now too.) She told me that it meant beautiful and that I was beautiful, but not only on the outside. She said that it was her term for me for all the beauty I possessed inside—some of it yet to be brought out into the world.

So, my dearest daughter, I shall call you Bella—for I know that you are a true beauty, inside and out—preparing to live a life that is full of love and happiness.

That's my wish for you, my sweet Bella.

I love you more than you could ever know.

Your Mother,
Arianna Sinclair

Isabella jumped when she heard her phone ding on the table beside her. She felt shivers up and down her spine when she saw who it was from.

Her father.

She smiled as she opened the text to read it.

A NOTE FROM THE AUTHOR

Thank you so much for reading *All in Good Time*.

If you've fallen in love with these characters and the world of the Legacy Series, I'd love to invite you deeper into the story.

I've written a quiet, emotional prequel titled *Out of Time* that sheds light on the relationships, choices, and moments that shaped everything that follows.

As a thank-you for joining my reader list, you can receive *Out of Time* as a free digital gift, along with future updates and special releases from the Legacy Series and my other women's fiction.

To receive your free prequel, please visit:
PaulaKayBooks.com

I'm so glad you're here.
—Paula

ABOUT THE AUTHOR

Paula Kay writes women's fiction about family, friendship, and the quiet moments that shape who we become.

Her Legacy Series explores love, loss, and the ties that bind us across generations, with settings inspired by Italy, San Francisco, and the places that feel like home long after we've left them behind.

When she's not writing, Paula enjoys meaningful conversations, books that make her cry, and a little too much reality television.

PaulaKayBooks.com

ALSO BY PAULA KAY

Legacy Series:

Book 1: *Buying Time*

Book 2: *In Her Own Time*

Book 3: *Matter of Time*

Book 4: *Taking Time*

Book 5: *Just in Time*

Book 6: *All in Good Time*

Book 7: *Bella's Hope*

Book 8: *Bella's Holiday*

Book 9: *Bella's Heart*

Book 10: *Bella's Home*

Book 11: *Christmas in Tuscany: A Legacy Series Reunion*

Book 12: *Birthday Surprise: A Legacy Series Reunion*

Book 13: *A Summer Together: A Legacy Series Reunion*

Book 14: *In This Moment: A Legacy Series Reunion*

Book 15: *Where It Began: A Legacy Series Reunion*

The Nomadic Sisterhood:

Know by Heart

Stay the Course

Clear the Air

Lost for Words

Out of Touch

Turn the Tide

Rock the Boat

Back on Track